SHAMELESS

THE MARRIAGE MAKER BOOK SIX THE RULES OF REFINEMENT

TARAH SCOTT

ERIN RYE

This is a Scarsdale Voices romance and is part of *The Marriage Maker* series written by Sue-Ellen Welfonder and Tarah Scott

ISBN-13: 978-0-9972146-9-7
ISBN-10: 0-9972146-9-4

www.scarsdalepublishing.com

Cover design by dreams2media & R. Jackson Designs
Editor Casey Yager

First Trade Paperback Printing by Scarsdale Publishing 2018

10 9 8 7 6 5 4 3 2

SP

RULES OF REFINEMENT

Noblemen aren't always honorable... but a rake is always charming

In a narrow lane off Edinburgh's illustrious Charlotte Square, stands a town house that is not quite as impressive as nearby residences, but remains a place of distinction. An air of quiet dignity is maintained by the courtyard that fronts the street, while privacy is assured by a wrought-iron gateway. This house is Lady Peddington's School for Young Ladies and is owned and run by Lady Honoria Peddington.

Girls fortunate enough to attend the academy are instructed in all aspects of proper comportment with emphasis on the importance of a pleasing demeanor and appearance, grace and good manners, the skills a lady needs to run a large, well-to-do household, and – of course - the necessity and advantages of an impeccable reputation. Scandal, the girls are warned, must be avoided at all costs.

Lady Peddington's own reputation is the finest, and all Edinburgh considers her above reproach. She is especially well-loved by the affluent merchants and lesser gentry who live on the fringes of the city's New Town where she operates her school. These clients appreciate her knack at finding affluent husbands for their daughters. No one suspects that her knowledge of men comes from the long-ago days when she wasn't Lady Honoria Peddington, but simply Honey Pedding who ran a well-doing Glasgow brothel.

Those skills, though secret, still serve her well, for when her school's famed graduation balls fail to secure suitable husbands for some of her more high-spirited girls, other gentlemen come to the fore, eager to accept these gems as pampered mistresses. So, however a girl's heart might lean, Lady Peddington's School for Young Ladies guarantees happiness for all.

CHAPTER 1

What More Could a Girl Ask For?

JULIA SQUINTED AGAINST THE LATE MORNING SUN THAT streamed through the open window behind Lady Honoria Peddington's study desk. Girlish laughter wafted up from the modest courtyard as Honoria rose then skirted the large, claw-footed mahogany desk to where Juliet stood on the dark green, paisley-patterned carpet. For a woman nearing fifty, Honoria was remarkably beautiful, with only the barest hint of gray in her red hair.

She pinned Juliet with a critical stare. "Curl your locks into *proper* ringlets for tonight."

"Tonight—" Juliet broke off when Honoria brushed one of the locks with her fingers.

"I want to see candlelight dance off those gold streaks." Honoria began a slow walk around Juliet, as if inspecting a horse she wished to purchase.

With the real Lady Peddington making her circuit, Juliet

stared at the large oil portrait of Lady Peddington that graced the mantle. At her back, hung a collection of small portraits of the local nobles of Edinburgh. She imagined the lords' collective 'tsk, tsks' as Honoria reached Juliet's face and grasped Juliet's chin, tilting her head sideways. "Stain your lips a darker shade of red. Your pout will drive him wild."

Him?

Her heartbeat accelerated.

Honoria released her. "And line your lower eyelashes. Your blue eyes are one of your best features." She stepped back and crossed her arms. "You will meet the Duke of Hamilton tonight at the Midnight Ball."

"Midnight Ball—the Duke of Hamilton?" Anger twisted through her, followed by fear. Of all things the headmistress and founder of Lady Peddington's School for Young Ladies could have thrown at her, Juliet hadn't imagined this.

"So, the notorious Duke of Hamilton intends to make me his mistress?" Juliet forced a smile and added with a double dose of sarcasm, "Why, Auntie Honoria, what more could a woman want?"

"Little, indeed," she said, ignoring Juliet's derision.

"Surely, you remember that I am returning to London in the morning," Juliet said. "I have no time for balls—or dukes."

Honoria pinned her with a stare. "I did not insist you attend the first ball, but I must insist you attend this one."

"Only gentlemen looking for less-than-honorable associations attend your Midnight Balls. You know that isn't what I want."

"There is nothing dishonorable about an agreement between adults," Honoria replied unruffled. "The duke will expect you at midnight. He is not a man who likes to be kept waiting."

Her heart sank. The Duke of Hamilton. His portrait did not hang on the wall alongside the illustrious nobility of Edinburgh. Still, Juliet had heard of the man. Who hadn't? His reputation preceded him. He was daring, handsome, scandalously rich and, "He's never stayed with a woman longer than six months," Juliet finished her thought out loud.

"There is a first time for everything," Lady Peddington said.

Lady Honoria Peddington wasn't truly her aunt, but she was the closest thing Juliet had to a relative. Auntie started her career in the same brothel as Juliet's mother, where they'd formed a sisterly bond. As the years passed, both women had fulfilled their dreams. Honoria Peddington—born Honey Pedding—relocated to Edinburgh and opened Lady Peddington's School for Young Ladies. Juliet's mother moved to London and opened Lady Aphrodite's House of Pleasure—Juliet's childhood home.

Honoria smiled gently. "There is no harm in meeting the man."

"I'm no fool," Juliet snapped. She nodded at the open window where her fellow students giggled in the small courtyard below. "*They* might not know the dangers of a Midnight Ball, but they don't have a madam for a mother, now, do they?"

"My *dearest* child," Lady Peddington rapped her knuckles sharply on the desk at her side, "lower your voice. We cannot have such words overheard."

Juliet huffed another breath, but replied in hushed tones, "I am not staying in Edinburgh, Auntie. I leave early for London."

Honoria gave her a shrewd look. "You are no more anxious to return home now than you were yesterday."

Juliet's heart constricted. Her aunt spoke the truth. She felt more at home here than anywhere else she'd ever lived. The year had passed too quickly. Juliet tossed a wistful glance at the bookshelves filled with leather-bound volumes of deportment and etiquette. She'd read them all—or tried to. Truth be told, they'd put her to sleep better than any posset ever had.

She had a plan to avoid the fate awaiting her in her mother's house. She'd spent the school year fostering relationships with young ladies who would soon head households of their own. They would need a dressmaker. She intended to convince her mother to let her attempt to become a dressmaker before being forced into life as a courtesan.

Juliet met her aunt's gaze. "Why meet this gentleman just as I'm leaving, Auntie Honey—Honoria?" After a year, she still slipped. "Have you sold my virginity to the highest bidder?"

Her mother had attempted just that the year before. She'd auctioned Juliet off to a middle-aged banker, a man with a stomach the size of a bull's, who smelled like one, too. She'd narrowly avoided the man's bed by convincing her mother a year at Lady Peddington's school would allow her to charge twice the amount from better-paying clientele.

Juliet realized Lady Peddington was talking.

"...caught Sir Stirling's eye, Juliet. He specifically requested that you attend tonight's ball and meet the duke."

Juliet frowned. "Sir Stirling James?" She'd seen the man only once, and from a great distance. One of the instructors had pointed him out during a sanctioned holiday outing in Edinburgh as he'd dashed past in a brightly polished carriage. "Where might he have seen me? When? How? I've followed the rules, Auntie Honoria. I've told no one *anything*." How could she? Classmates would faint from shock should they discover she'd been raised in a brothel. A new thought struck and she dropped her voice into an even lower whisper, "He isn't one of Mother's patrons, is he?"

"Heavens, no." She shook her head vigorously. "Nothing like that."

"Then why would he wish to make me a duke's *mistress?*" Juliet hissed.

"I'm not at all certain, child," Lady Peddington whispered. She nodded at the open window and waited for more giggles to drift through before adding, "Sir Stirling is an old friend—not that kind of old friend," she quickly added when Juliet opened her mouth to ask that very question. Her aunt gave her a knowing look. "You have behaved yourself here in Edinburgh, but what of London?"

Juliet winced inwardly. Oh. *London.* "I've been the picture of propriety, Auntie, I swear it," she lied.

After all, what did the pesky word 'propriety' actually *mean*? Everyone she'd met held a slightly different opinion on the matter. And really, who was to say that sneaking into London parties uninvited in order to frequent the card tables was truly improper? She'd been careful to wear a Venetian mask to protect her identity. After all, she'd met more than one gambler in the brothel while growing up. They'd taught her a good many card tricks over the years. Why *shouldn't* she put such knowledge to use? She'd been quite the mysterious and popular figure in London that summer, and she'd won a tidy sum— almost enough money to open her own dress shop. Almost.

"What have you done, child?" her aunt pressed.

"Nothing," she lied again.

Honoria's stare seemed to penetrate clear to her soul. "Did you, by chance, fall in love in London or—"

Juliet rolled her eyes. "Really, how can you ask? *Love* is a word thrown about too easily. I'm of no mind to lift my skirts for any man. Ever."

Her aunt chuckled as if relieved.

Juliet lifted a suspicious brow. "I still feel as if I've been sold as your prized cow."

"Nonsense. Sir Stirling is a matchmaker."

"Let him make a match elsewhere." Juliet tossed her head and turned to go.

"Juliet, listen to me."

Juliet paused, then faced Honoria.

Her aunt stepped forward. "Your blood runs hot, *too* hot for just any man. Mind you, I know. You should embrace that passion. Indeed, you'll blossom under the right man's touch. If the rumors about Duke Hamilton are true—"

"No, thank you," Juliet snapped.

"Think of it," her aunt whispered, eyes alight with anticipation. "A duke's mistress. A man of the duke's wealth would provide you not only a private house, but a yearly allowance, as well. Even your mother never dreamt *that* high for you."

Alarm coursed through Juliet. "You haven't told Ma, have you?" the words shot out before she could stop them.

Too late, Juliet realized her mistake. A calculating gleam entered Lady Peddington's eye. Juliet's heart sank. She'd just handed her aunt victory on a silver platter. There was no recovering now. Honoria knew Juliet would do anything to prevent her mother from gaining knowledge of the duke's interest.

"Let's strike a bargain," Juliet surrendered.

A smile twitched the older woman's mouth. "Have I taught you so little this year? A lady never bargains like a fishwife."

Juliet tossed her aunt a pleading look. "I'll do as you ask. I'll attend this Midnight Ball and dance with this duke. I'll entertain him, just as you wish—outside of bedding him. But mother can't know. *Please*, Auntie Honoria."

Lady Peddington primly took her seat. "Sir Stirling specifically requested that you play a game of commerce with the duke, and that you must win."

Cards? Juliet blinked. So, Sir Stirling *had* seen her at the London parties…but how had he recognized her? She'd always worn a mask. Heavens, had he had her followed? Horror washed over her.

"You should know," her aunt continued, "the Duke of Hamilton never loses."

Juliet took a deep fortifying breath and pushed her worries aside. "Until now," she replied. She hadn't lost a game in years —not with the tools she had at her disposal.

Lady Peddington smiled. "Keep the man happy. It's only one night. Do that, and your meeting with the duke shall remain our secret."

"Bless you." Juliet heaved a sigh of relief.

She left the study quickly. Oh, Honey Pedding was a wily one. She had manipulated the conversation in order to get her way. Juliet grimaced. She'd been raised by such women. How had she fallen so neatly into the net?

At the bottom of the stairs, she paused and peered out the window at the young ladies who still chatted in the courtyard. In the past week, most had found suitors, honorable men offering marriage—not dukes looking for mistresses. As a fresh bout of giggles erupted from the girls, Juliet shook her head. They knew little of men. She'd seen enough men in her mother's brothel to know them for the creatures they truly were: simple-minded fools focused solely on carnal pleasure.

The Duke of Hamilton would prove no different. She would play that lust to her advantage. She would wear her finest gown. She'd flirt, lick her lips, heave her breasts, and flash her ankles. Expose a little flesh and she could make the duke's blood boil. In a blink, she'd have him thinking with his cock. Then, she'd trounce him at cards, take his money and vanish.

CHAPTER 2

A Most Interesting Wager

"T HERE'S NO WOMAN ALIVE WHO CAN KEEP MY INTEREST LONG enough for me to want to marry her, Stirling."

Carrick Hamilton, Duke of Hamilton and Lord of Lennoxlove House, stood on the edge of the lawn, nocked an arrow to his longbow and took aim. The bowstring thrummed, and the arrow buried itself in the center of the target over a hundred yards away.

Sir Stirling James, Marquess of Roxburgh, who lounged under an ancient oak, let out a low whistle. "Impressive."

Carrick set his bow onto a nearby table, beside a collection of daggers, bows, and arrows—anything he could throw at a target. The sun was warm, the sky blue, the wind, nonexistent. All in all, a perfect day for target practice at Crenshaw House. So, why was he struggling with a dark mood? Perhaps, he should cut his Edinburgh visit short and return home. He stretched the kinks from his neck, then raked his dark hair back off his forehead.

"What were you saying? Ah, yes. Women." Carrick frowned. "Why are we speaking of women?"

"I said, you simply haven't met the right one." An amused twinkle lit Stirling's eyes.

Carrick snorted a laugh. "I'd wager my prize stallion there is no 'right' woman for the likes of me."

"I'll take that wager." Stirling grinned. "I'll back it with that red roan you've been lusting after."

Carrick shot his friend a startled look. "You're not jesting."

"Indeed, I am not," Stirling replied. "I've already found *her.*"

Carrick lifted a brow. He'd been after Stirling to sell him that red roan for two years. He leaned a hip against the weaponry table and crossed his arms. "Who is she?"

Stirling left the shade of the tree and joined him. "Marrying her will be rather tricky."

Carrick straightened. "Marry? Och, this is a jest, after all."

"Believe me, this is one you'll want to marry," Stirling assured. "Never have I seen a more perfect match."

Carrick grimaced. "Marriage?" He reclaimed his longbow and selected another arrow. "Duty dictates that I someday marry, but I don't see that happening anytime soon." He nocked the arrow and aimed.

Stirling laughed. "What you need is a woman who will bring you to your knees."

Carrick's shot went wild.

Stirling grinned and clapped him on the back. "I look forward to seeing your stallion in my stables." He spun on his heel and headed toward the house.

Carrick frowned. "When shall I meet this harridan?"

"Tonight," Stirling called over his shoulder. "At Lady Peddington's Midnight Ball."

A *Midnight Ball?* Carrick considered. Stirling had saved the most delightful surprise for last. He grinned. Aye, he was in the mood to spend the evening with a woman—especially one who attended midnight balls.

CHAPTER 3

A Game of Cards Like No Other

THE CLOCK ON THE BEDCHAMBER MANTLE CHIMED THE MIDNIGHT hour.

Juliet yanked her gaze from the book she'd been reading onto the clock. The Midnight Ball had begun. She set the book on the settee and rose. A tingle of anxiety climbed her spine. If even one of her friends lingered in the ballroom after the regular ball ended, the illusion she'd worked so hard to create this last year would shatter into a thousand pieces. Word would spread like wildfire and no one would hire the woman in the low-cut blue silk gown and Venetian mask as their dressmaker.

One way or another, this would be the last time she stood in this room. Juliet turned in a slow circle and inspected at the room, now empty of all signs that she had lived here for a year. Her gaze caught on a sliver of dark blue velvet at the foot of her bed. She crossed the room and scooped up the fabric. A scrap that had fallen to the floor when she'd packed the remnants she'd collected from the sewing they'd done at the school. Most pieces were only large enough to use as samples, but a few very nice pieces would suffice to make gloves or even reticules. Every little bit counted.

The money she'd saved would pay for just enough fabric and supplies to get started as a dressmaker. She didn't have a penny for room and board, but one didn't worry about such small details. Juliet grimaced. All she had to do was talk her mother into letting her live at the brothel until she could afford a modest home of her own. Until then, she had arranged to pay a small portion of her earnings to a shop owner in the fabric district for a place to meet with her clients. But her plans and future depended on her having a safe place to do her sewing.

Juliet released a sigh. The year really had passed too quickly. She loved her mother, but she wasn't looking forward to the battle that lay ahead. Her trunk awaited her atop the hired carriage that would take her to the coach headed for London. The day dress she would wear for the carriage ride home lay tucked in the satchel by the door. Once she escaped the duke, she dared not risk even a change of clothes in her room. The transformation from courtesan to dull dressmaker would take place in the carriage ride between Lady Peddington's and the depot.

Two girls at the school were already engaged to moderately successful London merchants and had begged Juliet to sew each of them full wardrobes. She would earn slave wages, but the girls would tell everyone that Miss Juliet Thatcher, graduate of Lady Peddington's School for Young Ladies, had sewn their dresses. Then her mother would have no good arguments to prevent her from becoming a dressmaker instead of a courtesan.

Juliet crossed to the full-length mirror near the door and inspected her appearance. The blue silk cradled her ample breasts to perfection and accentuated her thin waist. She tilted her head. Per Aunt Honoria's instructions, she'd darkened her lashes and lined her eyes. The dramatic effect made her blue eyes stand out under the mass of curls she'd swept back from her face and fastened in place with two large tortoiseshell combs—all but one seductive tendril, of course. She let it coil gracefully down the back of her neck like a careless afterthought. Men liked that kind of thing. It made them itch to entwine it around their finger.

Her gaze caught on her bodice as she started to turn, and she paused. She should lower the bodice another half inch. The dress was scandalous enough as it was—which meant she had nothing to lose. She tugged the bodice down

She couldn't help a humorless laugh. She looked like a pale ghost asleep on her feet. *That* wouldn't do. A mental image of herself snoring at the card tables made her grimace. If only she had the courage to defy Lady Peddington and her mother. She nibbled on her lip. Not bloody likely. The force of their personalities alone was daunting. But that wasn't the real reason. In truth, she knew they only sought to give her an easier life than they'd had. She suppressed a sigh and pinched her cheeks to bring out the roses.

The distant strains of a waltz filtered into the room.

She could delay no longer.

Juliet reached for the deck of cards she'd set on the mantle. She'd filched them from the card rooms earlier in the day. She removed the aces along with the face cards and tucked them into a small pouch hanging from a garter on her thigh.

Next, she picked up the Venetian mask, a dainty white satin oval trimmed with white feathers and gold piping just large enough to cover her nose and brows. She wasn't attending a masked ball, but she knew how to tease a man. Juliet fluffed the feathers, tied the ribbons behind her head, and twirled in front of the mirror one last time. The gloves had to go. It was Lady

Peddington's Midnight Ball, after all. That meant bare flesh. She stripped off the gloves and draped them over the back of the settee.

At last, she was ready—as ready as she would ever be.

"Prepare to be stunned, Duke of Hamilton." She gave a lofty wave of her hand, gathered her skirts, swept out the door and down the stairs. She paused in the downstairs foyer, outside the ballroom.

Juliet had witnessed years of scandalously grand entrances at the brothel. A tantalizing amount of skin, a seductive sway of the hips, and a devil-may-care attitude were the main requirements of a successful entrance. With one final downward tug at her bodice, she lifted her head and swooped through the door.

Few candles burned, leaving the corners of the ballroom shrouded in intentional darkness. The girls who waltzed were cradled closely in their partners' arms. She recognized a few of the men from the portraits that hung on the wall of her aunt's study. The Duke of Hamilton's ancestral lands lay north of Edinburgh, which is why his portrait didn't hang on the wall. What had brought him to Edinburgh? Her ill luck, is what. Her gaze drifted to the refreshment table hugging the wall to the right. Bouquets of spring flowers tastefully encircled silver bowls of Aunt Honoria's special midnight punch.

No one approached her. There could be only one reason for that: the duke had warned all others off. That he made her wait at the door spoke volumes. He was obviously a man of command, accustomed to getting his way. No doubt, women tripped over their feet and drooled after him. Their mistake. A man of his power lived for the thrill of the chase.

Well, it was time to see him run.

With a proud toss of her head, Juliet turned on her heel and quit the room. She'd gone three steps when strong fingers closed around her arm. She suppressed a smile. So easily snared. Juliet paused and, brow arched, slowly faced the man.

By God, he was handsome. Devastatingly so. He wore his dark chestnut hair longer than current fashion dictated, but it suited him. The fabric of his expensively-tailored, velvet cutaway coat stretched across the defined muscles of his chest. She dropped a slow gaze, mimicking the best of Lady Aphrodite's girls in a bold inspection of his lean hips and the tight breeches that hugged muscled thighs. Juliet deliberately lingered on his groin before lifting her gaze to the details of his expertly tied cravat, smoothly shaven chin, and the regal curve of his lips. Her pulse quickened. She hadn't realized how heated the 'Lady Aphrodite Inspection' could make the originator. She shook the feeling aside and concentrated on her prey. Small wonder women found him attractive. He was quite the specimen.

Finally, she lifted her lashes and looked into a pair of piercing gray—and vastly amused—eyes.

"You must be the ravishing Juliet," the duke said in a deep baritone. "Please allow me to introduce myself. I am Carrick Hamilton."

"Carrick," she repeated his name in low, sultry tones, and graced him with a slight nod. He'd hear no 'my lords' or 'sirs' escape her lips.

"Shall we dance?" Slowly, he slid his fingers down her elbow and over her bare forearm before dropping his hand away.

The simple gesture left a trail of fire in its wake. No matter. She had a trap of her own to set; a man to keep intrigued and off balance.

As he offered his arm and nodded toward the ballroom door, she boldly stepped into his arms—much closer than propriety allowed—and murmured, "I would much prefer to waltz here."

Delight danced in his eyes. He crushed her so close, the

buttons on his waistcoat pressed into the soft mounds of her breasts as he began to twirl her in the dimly lit hallway. The flex of hard muscle against her softness startled her. His fingers drifted lower to the swell of her hip. Heat radiated off his broad chest. Juliet shoved aside the distraction. She had a game to play.

"I do love a waltz," Juliet said *sotto voce* as she peered up at him through her Venetian mask.

"By Jove, Stirling was right." His chest vibrated with a deep chuckle. "You're quite beautiful."

It was an easy opening. She'd witnessed her mother's girls spar in provocative wordplay countless times and summoned a mischievous smile. "Beautiful? Beauty is merely the cover of the book, is it not? Is not what lies underneath more...interesting?" She punctuated the question by mimicking Lady Aphrodite's most popular girl's signature move: a flutter of the lashes combined with a slow, undulating arch of the back.

The rub of her breasts against the solid wall of his muscled chest hardened her nipples. A shock of sensation rippled straight to her core. She drew a startled breath.

The man studied her through hooded eyes. "I believe you would be a book worth reading, my dear." He executed an expert turn. "Perhaps, even more than once."

Perhaps? That smacked of an insult.

"I fear I may be written in a language you cannot understand." She flashed her eyes.

With a devious quirk of his lip, he trailed a slow finger up her spine. She couldn't halt the shiver of response. He felt it. He couldn't miss it. Not with how tightly he held her.

He lowered his head and whispered in her ear, "There's only one language between a man and a woman, my dear. And yes, I read it astonishingly well, in all its forms."

The situation wasn't proceeding as planned. The man obviously knew a few tricks of his own. She'd been taught that suggestive innuendo drove men mad with desire—she hadn't realized it worked the other way, as well. As he twirled her again, she decided it was time to play a different game, and gracefully slipped free of his arms.

"Where are you going?" He fell into step beside her as she glided toward the ballroom.

Juliet lifted her chin and fixed him with a cool stare. "Perhaps, this book doesn't wish to be read, Carrick."

Their gazes locked. She couldn't deny the strong tug of attraction this time. He obviously felt it, too.

He looked away first, then performed a lazy assessment of her slender form. "On the contrary, my dear, this book is simply begging to be explored."

The lust on his face sent her pulse soaring. She couldn't allow him to get the upper hand. This was a game. Nothing more. She curved her lips in an ambiguous smile and turned away.

The musicians struck the opening notes of another waltz as she stepped through the ballroom door and paused inside.

A balding man immediately emerged from the nearby shadows and bowed low. "May I have this—"

"No, you may not." Carrick clamped a possessive hand around her waist.

She hid a smile. As expected, like a puppet on *her* string, he'd followed her.

The man scurried away like a frightened rabbit.

This time, Carrick didn't ask permission. With smooth, elegant grace, he caught her close and spun her onto the ballroom floor, locking her against his powerful body with a hand placed low on the small of her back.

For several long moments, she surrendered to the foreign desire to mold herself against him. They whirled in the glittering candlelight, easily weaving through the remaining couples on the dance floor. As they spun into a darkened corner, Carrick's hand slid across her buttocks until they emerged into the light once again.

Juliet had expected as much, but instead of feeling affronted, she wondered what his lips would feel like on her naked skin. Somehow, the thought didn't evoke the same disgust it did when observing the clientele in her mother's establishment.

"A penny for your thoughts," the whispered words bathed her ear with warm breath.

Her heart beat fast. Might he nuzzle her ear? He didn't—of course. The man was clearly a master of seduction and, much to her chagrin, he'd won the game—so far. But all was not lost.

Juliet lowered her lashes and, with a naughty little smile, slid the tip of her tongue along the upper seam. "Perhaps, I wished that I danced with the other gentleman."

Was it her imagination or did his muscular arm flinch? It was difficult to tell. The gray eyes looking down at her only held a wry amusement.

"No doubt, if you wished to dance with the fellow, you would be doing so."

Again, he whirled her into a darkened corner and, this time, stopped and slid his hands lower until he cupped her buttocks. Excitement thrilled through her as he gently undulated his hard length against her.

"Tell me what you wish, Juliet." He nuzzled the sensitive skin under her ear.

His body fascinated her. She liked how her name sounded like a song when he said it.

What she wished? His question suddenly roused her from the haze of lust. She knew what she wanted. She'd thought of nothing else the past three years. She wished to become a dressmaker—though one wouldn't guess it who watched her in the ballroom's shadows with a man's hardened cock pressed against her abdomen.

That realization evoked a perverse grin even as shock twisted through her. She'd come close to proving her aunt right. She *was* too hot-blooded for her own good. But then... her passionate blood had served her well. She had the man right where she wanted him: thinking with his cock.

Now, it was time to play cards, and, judging by his thick erection, she might not need to cheat.

Juliet slipped free of his embrace. He groaned, and her smile widened. He reached for her, but she avoided his grasp with a quick sideways step. She tossed her head, adjusted the ribbons of her mask, and started toward the card room, which opened off the far end of the ballroom.

She didn't wonder if Carrick followed. She knew he did.

The card room's gaming tables boasted half a dozen gentlemen sipping brandy and lounging on plush green chairs with their legs splayed wide. The men sat up straighter as she entered, but she ignored them and angled toward a table in the darkest corner of the room. The shadows would aid her if cheating proved necessary.

Juliet took the seat with the wall at her back and the door facing. Carrick entered and paused. Her heart beat wildly as he scanned the room. She deftly adjusted her skirts, withdrew the cards she'd tucked in the garter's hidden pouch, and slipped them under her seat cushion as his gaze settled on her.

Eyes locked on her face, he strode across the room.

"Join me," she invited in a low voice when he arrived, and she picked up the deck of cards resting on the table. "A game of commerce, shall we? Three rounds."

"What shall we wager?" He sat down sideways in his seat and stretched out his long legs.

Her throat went dry. Dear God, the man knew what he was about. The blatant lust in his eyes held her mesmerized. For the first time in her life, her pulse raced at the thought of a man touching her most intimate places and suckling her tender flesh. Wet heat pooled between her thighs.

It took a moment to recall he'd asked a question. Juliet frowned. How had she succumbed to his designs yet again? Irritation flared. She inhaled a mind-clearing breath and dropped her gaze to the cards. It was time to turn the tables on the man and his seductive ways.

With deliberate focus, she leaned forward to provide him an unimpeded view of cleavage as she fanned the cards in a line and ran her fingertips sensuously over the patterned, gold-painted backs. Juliet repressed a grimace. She'd tugged her bodice so low, she could only hope her breasts didn't escape the confines of her gown.

"What should we wager?" she asked with a little aching pant, mimicking the sound her mother's girls used to drive men wild. She followed with the standard sucking in of her bottom lip. Slowly, she let her lip drag against her teeth, then released it, and added, "Gentlemen first."

He watched her. "I would see you…uncovered." His piercing gray eyes flicked to her mask before sliding down to her breasts.

Her heart skipped a salacious beat and she flirted with the idea of losing—but only for a moment. She gathered the cards and cut the deck with a one-handed pivot cut.

His eyes lit with appreciation. "And your bet?"

It was time to stack the deck. For that, she needed a distraction. She dropped her eyes to his necktie and murmured, "Your cravat. I…would…claim it."

"Are you in the habit of collecting men's cravats?" he queried softly.

She offered a mysterious smile, then dealt the hand. She set the deck to her right then reached for her cards. He grasped her wrist. She glanced up, surprised.

"One round," he demanded in a rough voice.

One round? She would definitely have to cheat.

"Very well," she agreed.

Juliet slid her palm over her cards in a lover's caress and, as his gaze tracked her fingers, she dropped her other hand to retrieve the aces from under the cushion.

His gaze lifted from the fingers skimming the cards to her face. Her breath hitched when the fire in his eyes intensified. She took another stuttered breath and her bodice felt as if it would burst. He shifted in his seat and her nipples pebbled. He couldn't possibly *see* her nipples through her corset. Still, she had to will her trembling fingers into submission when she quickly brushed one palm over the other, skillfully exchanging the cards.

"Shall we?" This time, she only half-feigned her shallow breathing as she tapped the table with her knuckles, signaling time to display their cards.

Carrick's gray eyes caught and held hers as he slowly placed his cards face-up on the table. Four kings. She blinked, her long lashes brushing her mask. He had cheated! She hadn't noticed a thing. Well, that would teach her to watch the man. With a private smile, she rose.

He lifted a curious brow.

"Do not move," she ordered in low, throaty tones. "I would fetch my prize."

Curiosity crossed his face as she walked around the table, trailing a finger along the linen-covered table. She stopped behind him. He smelled of sandalwood and pure masculinity and, damn him, the way his coat stretched over his broad shoulders captured her attention too easily. Heart pounding, Juliet placed the heels of her palms on his broad shoulders and let the cards slide from her hands and down his chest. Two of the aces landed face up on his thighs. The other two landed in his crotch. God help her.

His muscled chest rose and fell.

Slowly, she slipped her fingers around his neck. He tilted his head back against the pillow of her breasts and closed his eyes. Juliet shivered. He inhaled a deep breath. It took longer than she'd expected to untie his cravat—Lady Aphrodite's girls had made it seem so easy—but at last, the deed was done.

With a sensuous twist of her wrist, she slid the silk free and stepped back. "Thank you, Carrick, for a most pleasant evening."

She turned away and heard the harsh intake of his breath followed by the scrape of his chair. She quickened pace when his bootfalls followed, but she eluded him by slipping into the shadows, then made a quick righthand turn out a side door and up the Servant stairs. She was glad to go. Midnight balls were far too dangerous—especially for girls like her.

CHAPTER 4

Smitten

CARRICK TOOK THE STAIRS TWO AT A TIME, THEN SUCKED IN A sharp breath as Juliet vanished into the darkness as if she'd been a ghost. He slowed. He'd break his fool neck if he wasn't careful. He reached the next floor, where meager hallway candlelight gave way to total darkness. His heart thudded. By God, he wanted to kiss her. Never had he played a more sensuous game of cards. The way she'd caressed the deck made him need to feel those slim fingers wrapped around his cock. And the way she'd teased him with her delicate, pink tongue? He was determined to taste those gorgeous lips and ravish them. His body tightened at the thought.

She'd obviously cheated with those four aces. It only made him want her more. He needed her—no, he needed to conquer her.

He stormed back down the stairs and made a thorough search of every darkened corner of the ballroom, demanding every candle and lamp be lit until the place stood bathed in light as bright as day.

As he feared, she had truly disappeared.

Finally, he thundered at a waiter, "Find Lady Peddington. Rouse her from her bed, if necessary. I must speak with her at once."

LADY PEDDINGTON TOLD CARRICK NOTHING SAVE THAT JULIET had left for London. He left the school headed for Stirling's home, then got halfway and realized it was nearly three in the morning. With a curse, he ordered his driver to take him home.

At noon, he knocked on Stirling's townhouse and was shown into the parlor. While he paced, a maid brought tea and, minutes later, Stirling entered the room.

"This is a pleasant surprise, Carrick." He shook Carrick's hand. "Tea?" Stirling seated himself on the divan.

"Nae," Carrick said.

Stirling frowned. "You look harried. Is something wrong?"

"I suspect you know full well what is wrong," Carrick said in frustration.

Stirling filled a teacup, then sat back and took a sip.

The smirk Stirling didn't quite hide told Carrick he was right. "Where can I find her?"

"By 'her,' I assume you mean Miss Thatcher?"

"Thatcher." He threw himself into a nearby chair. "Juliet Thatcher." He pinned Stirling with a stare. "What do you know of her?"

"I received her portrait a week ago and recognized her, at once. I saw her at a London house party last year."

"What do you mean, 'received her portrait'?" Carrick demanded.

"A young lady at Lady Peddington's school asked for my help. She mentioned that three other friends were in the same predicament she was, that is, they hadn't found respectable gentlemen for husbands."

Carrick stared. "Surely, you don't think I'm respectable?"

"What is more respectable than a duke?" Stirling chuckled. "The lass is adept at card cheating, don't you agree?"

Carrick laughed. "She is a vixen."

Stirling grinned. "Sounds like a perfect match."

"Not if she's looking for a husband," he said. "Though, she certainly didn't act like a husband hunting lass. I took her for a courtesan."

"That's probably because her mother owns a very popular gentleman's establishment in London."

Carrick blinked. "You don't mean…"

Stirling nodded. "Aye, she owns an upscale brothel, Lady Aphrodite's House of Pleasure.

"How in God's name did Juliet end up at Lady Peddington's?" Carrick asked.

"She aspires to be a dressmaker."

Carrick stared. "You jest."

Stirling laughed. "Nae. Her mother has other ideas, however."

Carrick studied his friend. "You seem to know a great deal about her."

Stirling nodded and took another sip of tea, then set the cup on the table. "Lady Peddington and I are old friends. Miss Thatcher's mother intends to auction her off to the highest bidder."

"Bloody hell," Carrick cursed. "You aren't serious. You said she wanted to become a dressmaker."

"I also said her mother has other ideas."

Carrick shoved to his feet and started for the door.

"London is a long journey to make for just any woman," Stirling commented as Carrick headed for the door.

"Juliet Thatcher isn't just any woman." He reached the door

and paused to look back at his old friend. "Be warned, I still plan to collect that roan from you." With that, he quit the room.

THREE DAYS LATER, CARRICK REINED HIS HORSE TO A STOP ON A busy London street and hailed a man with prematurely thinning hair, a bulbous nose, and close-set eyes. "Can you direct me to Lady Aphrodite's House of Pleasure?" he asked.

The man grinned. "Aye, m'lord. About two miles down the main road." He pointed the way. "Turn onto the road with a brick townhouse and short, wrought iron gate. Then take the second alley to the right, mate. You can't miss it. There's a tall wrought iron gate in front of the house and a painting of the love goddess in the window." He hesitated, then added, "If I may say so, ask for Lucy. She's a wonder, that one is."

Carrick thanked the man and, half an hour later, he reached the narrow lane. A row of gray limestone houses hugged the street, each house looking very much like the one before, but as the man had said, only one domicile had a small but garish painting of Aphrodite propped in the window.

Carrick drew an exhilarating breath of crisp morning air. He'd found her. Anticipation coiled in his belly as he dismounted. The day he'd taken to wrap up his business in Edinburgh, along with the two-day ride to London, hadn't cooled his ardor. If anything, he wanted Juliet even more than he had. He would double any bids offered from other gentlemen—even if she'd already signed a contract.

He dismounted, tied his horse to the post, and went through the wrought iron gate and up the walk. He'd just stepped onto the porch and lifted his knuckles to rap on the door when it opened to reveal a long-haired, burly gentleman in gaily colored clothing.

"My lord, how may I be of service?"

"I've come to speak with the owner of this house," Carrick informed him coolly.

"Who shall I say is calling?"

"The Duke of Hamilton."

The door yanked wide and he locked gazes with a middle-aged matron with bright green eyes and ginger hair. Her body had been squeezed into a red, low-cut gown that artfully emphasized her curves.

"Come in, Your Grace." She offered a sweeping gesture followed by a low curtsey that offered a bird's eye view of her ample cleavage. "I'm Lady Aphrodite, the owner of this fine establishment."

Carrick ducked under the lintel and entered.

She turned to the butler and directed in a low voice, "Bring refreshments at once," then smiled up at Carrick. "Come, my lord. This way."

He followed her down a hall, where more paintings of Aphrodite adorned the walls, and past a large room where one beribboned, satin-clad young lady lounged on a settee. As he passed, the woman lazily lifted her fan and coquettishly dropped her lashes. Finally, they entered a small parlor. A large portrait of Aphrodite, painted in golds and crimson, matched the upholstery of the low couch and chaise lounge.

"Please, have a seat, my lord." She closed the door. "You look as if you've had a long journey. Would you care for brandy?"

He shook his head and sat down. "I'm looking for a Juliet Thatcher."

Surprise flickered in her eyes, but she quickly recovered and said, "May I ask why you are looking for our lovely Juliet?"

Why? She'd cast a net over him, that was why. For the first time in his life, he struggled to voice the words raging through his mind. "I have business to discuss with her."

"Our Juliet's not here," she said.

Relief flooded through him. It had been unlikely she would

have arrived ahead of him and signed a contract with another man so quickly, but the worry had niggled. "Even better," he said. "She will soon arrive, however. I seem to have outpaced the coach from Edinburgh."

"I see," she murmured. "Perhaps I could better help you if I understood the nature of your...business with Juliet."

Lust stormed through him. "Come, madam, we are neither of us naïve. Why else would a man ride from Edinburgh to London for a woman like Juliet?"

A calculated look appeared in her eyes. "You're interested in our Juliet?"

"I am—exclusively," he said, and wondered for the hundredth time what madness had seized him. He'd never set such a restriction on any other woman. "Draw up whatever contract you please," he said. "Price is of no concern. Make it for a month—maybe more."

She tilted her head. "Juliet is much more than a simple lady of Aphrodite, Your Grace." After a pregnant pause, she added, "She's my daughter."

He pinned her with an icy stare. "A mother who intended to auction her daughter off."

Most men squirmed under his stare. Juliet's mother stared back, unabashed. "My lord, surely, you do not condemn a woman for doing the very thing you are paying her to do?"

"Juliet is not *my* daughter," he replied.

"True." Her gaze sharpened. "Therefore, it is my place to ensure that she lives a comfortable life and has security as she ages. If you know a better way for a woman to accomplish that, I am ready to entertain your ideas."

Embarrassment flushed over him. "Forgive me, I overstepped my bounds."

She smiled, and Carrick saw where Juliet got her keen mind. "You're clearly a man with a healthy appetite," she said. "Just the sort of man my daughter needs. I'll see her treated fairly. And while Juliet is my daughter, she's also a lady of this house—or will be, after she's known a man's touch."

After she's known a man's touch? It took a moment for the meaning to sink through his haze of exhaustion and lust. Juliet was a virgin? *How?* She'd appeared well-versed in the arts of tantalizing a man. A wave of disappointment coursed through him. He'd thought to find an experienced lady of pleasure, one trained to slake his need. He didn't deflower virgins. Yet even as the thought swirled in his head, a primal hunger stirred his soul. Juliet, with her sultry voice, her mysterious blue eyes and long wave of gold-streaked hair…Juliet could be his and his alone.

"As the most sought-after lady in this house, the honor of taking her virginity has reached a princely sum," the woman was saying.

Carrick snapped from his thoughts. The most sought-after woman? "Nae," the word ripped from his mouth. "There will be no other."

A triumphant smile curved one corner of her mouth.

He locked gazes with her. "Nicely done, madam."

She angled her head in acknowledgement. "We are agreed then. A woman of her quality requires a house and a yearly allowance. I will not consider anything less than a year."

"Draw up a contract with your demands and have done," he said.

She rose. "Let me fetch the pen and parchment."

She sailed out the door and he leaned back to stretch his arms along the back of the couch. He needed a bath and a good night's sleep. Carrick released a breath. A virgin. God help him.

Movement near the door caught his attention and he glanced over as a woman entered. The winsome lass had long blonde curls and wore a beribboned shift thin enough to provide an enticing glimpse of her dark areolas and the patch of hair tucked at the apex of her thighs.

"Can I offer you anything while you wait, my lord?" She swayed her hips as she approached. "I'm Lucy."

Ah, the fair Lucy. He opened his mouth to send her away, then changed his mind. She *did* have something he needed. Desperately. He tapped his fingers along the back of the couch. "Join me."

She smiled, then settled by his side and reached for his crotch.

He caught her wrist. "Nae, lass, not that." He placed her hand firmly on her knee. "I simply wish to talk, my dear." He reached into his waistcoat, withdrew several pound notes and pressed them into her hand. He had a mistress to seduce, "I need you to tell me everything you know about Juliet."

CHAPTER 5

Home Again

JULIET YAWNED AND OPENED HER EYES. SHE SAT IN THE COACH, sandwiched between a large man who smelled like cheese and a frazzled woman travelling with four children—creatures, Juliet now suspected, that had been spawned in hell. Never had she seen a more unruly bunch. Through the coach window, she glimpsed the city of London spread over the horizon. At last. She was almost home.

There had been nothing else to do in the coach but think and, for the most part, she'd thought of little else but the Midnight Ball. She couldn't forget the tingle of Carrick's fingers as they'd trailed over her skin, a tantalizing touch she'd relived again and again the entire journey. Truth be told, she'd imagined much, much more, but with London only minutes away, she could no longer indulge in fantasies of those smoky gray eyes. More pressing matters awaited her. The most important being a mother to outwit before the woman again auctioned off her virginity.

Soon enough, the coach rolled over London's cobblestoned streets and stopped at the King's Head Inn. Juliet alighted into her mother's waiting and welcoming arms.

"It's so good to see you, love." Her mother hugged her close before holding her at arm's length. "You have lost weight."

"I'm fine, Ma," Juliet laughed, inspecting her mother in turn.

It had only been a year since they'd parted. Her mother looked very much the same as she always had, buxom and pleasing, with a pert nose, green eyes and red hair. Juliet with her dark locks and blue eyes had clearly taken after her father —whoever that might have been. Even her mother wasn't sure. They interrupted their greetings and stepped aside as an arrogant lady swept past, her maid in tow.

"Hoity-toity." Her mother rolled her eyes as the young woman swept out of sight. "I'd pity the man wed to that poor soul—if I didn't know he'd turn up at my door as a good-paying customer." She laughed.

Juliet offered a wry smile as one of her mother's hired men shoved her trunk onto the bed of a cart.

"Take the cart on up to the house," her mother ordered the man. "Juliet and I will walk. We must chat."

Chat? Juliet thinned her lips. "Ma, must we talk business so soon?"

Her mother's eyes narrowed into shrewd, calculating slits. "It's always time to talk business, Juliet. Especially now. I moved the ball up a week. It's tonight. I feared you wouldn't make it in time."

"*Tonight?*" Juliet repeated in dismay. She was sore, stiff, and tired from the journey, and she desperately needed a bath.

"You have a few hours, yet," her mother assured with a smile and a fond pat on the cheek. "You're young. You'll feel spry enough in no time. I set up your card table in the sitting room and you mustn't forget to wear your mask."

Cards. That was a relief. At least her mother hadn't auctioned her off—yet. "Well, as long as it's just playing cards, Ma," she gave in, but, unable to resist, added, "But we really need to talk about my career. Much has transpired since—"

"Come, come, we'll chat later," her mother interrupted with a smile.

The smile made Juliet stop in her tracks. Her mother invariably responded to all dressmaking overtures with theatrics—certainly never with a kindly, 'we'll chat later.'

"What have you done?" Juliet demanded.

"What have I done?" Her mother snorted, looped her arm through Juliet's, and pulled her down the street. "I've simply welcomed my daughter home. That's all. Now don't spare the bath oils, and wear your finest. We have a ball tonight: Lady Aphrodite's Night of Wonders."

The last thing Juliet wanted was to attend another ball, but at least she had one consolation. This time, she didn't have to deal with the disconcerting Duke of Hamilton. With a long, loud sigh, she followed her mother, wondering why that thought didn't conjure as much relief as it should.

Juliet gathered her silvery, gossamer silk skirts in one hand and proceeded out her room and down the stairs. Cut in the French fashion of forty years before, the voluminous skirts floated around her ankles, preventing her from seeing where she stepped. She nearly missed the bottom riser before she reached the floor and entered the crowded ballroom.

"Careful now," her mother called as she arrived.

Lady Aphrodite's Night of Wonders was well underway. Swirls of colorful silk and glittering glass jewelry met Juliet's eyes everywhere she looked as Lady Aphrodite's girls, their assets on full display, mingled with the clientele.

Brenda swooped over, grabbed Juliet's arm, and pointed toward the sitting room. "Your card table is ready." She giggled and dropped her gaze to Juliet's bosom. "But *you're* clearly not, love. Pull that gown lower and show more flesh." Brenda yanked Juliet's bodice. The edge of the fabric slid dangerously low over her nipples. "There." The girl nodded in satisfaction as Juliet fitted her mask over her face. "Your first customers have arrived." She escorted Juliet to the sitting room and urged her inside.

Juliet heaved a sigh. She really wasn't in the mood to play cards with a gaggle of pawing men. She glanced around the sitting room. Someone had decorated the mantle and tables with elaborate ivy and thistle garlands, elegantly tied in gold ribbon. Cheap, imitation Grecian pedestals bearing baskets of fruit and cheese lined the walls. A fire crackled in the grate behind a card table draped in white velvet. A man already lounged there, and several more waited nearby. Juliet scarcely gave them notice as she woodenly approached her chair and, after fluffing her cushion, took her seat with an unceremonious plop.

"A game of commerce for the gentleman?" she asked. She glanced up—and froze.

Carrick Hamilton's smoldering gray eyes stared back at her.

CHAPTER 6

What Lies Beneath

CARRICK WATCHED JULIET. SHE WORE THE SAME WHITE-feathered Venetian mask she'd worn three nights ago, and her breasts nearly spilled over the bodice of her deliciously enticing silver gown. His cock hardened in approval.

"Fancy meeting you again, Juliet," he drawled.

Her lips—such luscious lips—parted in shock.

Another man strolled across the room.

Carrick jolted from the spell. He rose and faced the other men. Merchants and laborers, for the most part. He knew how to deal with men of their ilk. "Gentlemen, I would like some privacy with the lady. Take your pick of the other women here, at my expense."

"I beg your pardon," Juliet said behind him.

"I beg your pardon?" one man echoed.

Two men came to their feet.

Another snorted and opened his mouth to object.

He nodded at the door. "Tell the lady of the house to send your bill to the Duke of Hamilton."

"Duke of Hamilton?" one man said. He looked at Juliet. "Is this man who he says he is?"

She remained mute.

Carrick imagined she wanted to condemn him to the darker parts of hell, but he kept his attention on the men. They exchanged glances with one another, then shrugged and filed from the room.

As the door clicked shut behind them, Carrick faced Juliet once more. His gaze caught on the hint of pink nipples peeking out of her gown. A flush of heat tightened his groin. He had to maintain his dignity. It was one thing to desire a prospective mistress, quite another to ogle her like a common doxy. He returned his gaze to her face. The blue eyes staring back at him through the mask had narrowed.

"I am pleased to see you again," he said.

She remained silent.

"Surely, you can't be surprised to see me after what transpired between us at the Midnight Ball, Juliet."

Something flickered in her eyes, but he couldn't read her expression through the damn mask. He'd had quite enough of the thing. He rounded the table in two strides and grasped the ribbon holding the mask in place. Juliet jerked, but he grasped her shoulder with one hand and tugged the tie free with the other. The white satin mask fell to the floor.

Juliet stiffened.

Carrick's breath caught. He'd known she was beautiful—after all, the silk creation hadn't hidden everything—but unmasked... Almond-shaped blue eyes held his gaze with an intensity that started his heart to hammer. Dark hair framed high cheekbones and flawless skin. He well understood how her mother had named the establishment after the goddess Aphrodite. He was powerless to look away.

"You're beautiful," he whispered.

Juliet blinked, her thick lashes fanning her cheeks. She shifted, as if to stand, but he whirled and returned to his chair.

"A game of commerce, shall we?" he murmured.

"I am not for sale, Carrick," she said in a fierce whisper. "You cannot just take my body."

"I'm not trying to, lass," he said.

Juliet snorted. "How did you find me? No doubt my aunt sold me out. Honoria doesn't know how to keep quiet."

Aunt? Lady Peddington? Interesting. "Your aunt told me nothing save that you had returned to your London home."

Her mouth thinned. "Why are you here?"

He pulled the contract from his inner vest pocket. Alarm crossed Juliet's face as her gaze fell to the parchment. With a grim twist of her mouth, she snatched it from his grasp and stared at the words.

Finally, she laid the paper on the table and rose. "I must speak with my mother."

He pushed to his feet and stepped into her path. "I won't force you, Juliet. I'm not that kind of a man."

"Won't force me? Then what is that?" She jabbed a finger at the contract.

"That is protection."

The eyes staring up at him were rife with suspicion. "Protection? From?"

They stood close, her breasts inches from his chest. The perfume of her hair swirled around him. "From me," he said. "This contract ensures you'll never do anything you do not wish to do."

Interest lit her eyes. "That includes bedding you?" At his nod, she added, "Of what possible advantage is such a contract to you when I've no intentions of letting you in my bed?"

"Time," he answered truthfully. "The contract buys me time to seduce my mistress."

Juliet laughed, a silvery sound filled with wry amusement. "I've seen it all in the brothel, Carrick. There isn't a trick I don't know."

He grinned. "Then you have nothing to lose, and everything to gain. I'll send my carriage around for you in the morning to take you to Lennoxlove House. My mother and sister are in sore need of a dressmaker."

She went ramrod stiff.

"Should you, indeed, prove impervious to my charms" –he flashed a smile— "sewing the gowns of the Dowager Duchess and her daughter will go far in establishing your reputation, will it not?"

She blinked. "Is this some sort of trick?"

He shook his head. "My mother and sister are in need of new dresses."

"They will be there?" she said, then added as if speaking more to herself than him, "That is very good," and he realized he'd erred. He hadn't intended on his mother and sister being at Lennoxlove House.

"The dowager duchess will not be pleased that her son has installed his mistress as her dressmaker," Juliet said.

"She will not be staying permanently."

"Neither will I," Juliet said. "I see the contract allows for a cottage of my choosing."

He angled his head in agreement. "Even here in London, if you choose."

Juliet pinned him with a stare. "You will tire of me before the year stipulated in the contract—especially when I keep turning you away."

He bent his head until his lips almost touched her ear. She stiffened, but didn't step away. "Shall we say I have until summer's end to...woo you?" Carrick drew back enough to see her face.

A calculating gleam –with a hint of amusement—lit her

blue eyes. "If I *manage* to resist your charms until the end of summer, you honor the contract for the year—the money and a cottage."

He nodded.

The gleam darkened. "I sew your sister's and mother's gowns?"

"Aye," he said.

"Done."

"Done," he agreed before she could recant.

"What if I lose?" she said.

His heart began to thud. "If you lose, my dear, I will have you."

Juliet laughed. "Shall we seal the agreement with a handshake?" She extended a hand.

Carrick locked gazes with her and clasped her smaller hand in his larger one. He took a step closer and looked down at her. "Have you the courage to seal the deal properly?"

Understanding flickered across her face and her eyes narrowed. She pulled her hand free of his and for one horrible instant he feared he'd miscalculated. Then she seized his lapel and dragged his mouth down to hers.

The instant their lips met, need rammed through him. She stiffened, and Carrick realized he'd crushed her to him. He loosened his hold and cupped her face with his right hand. Hope surged through him when he detected a tremor in her body. His heart soared. She wasn't as impervious to him as she thought. God help him, he wanted her badly.

She wasn't a doxy off the streets and this cardroom was no place to prove he could please her. Damn, she hadn't even signed the contract yet. He flicked her mouth with this tongue. His heart thundered. Would she allow him entrance? Juliet opened on a soft gasp and he plunged his tongue inside. He'd never tasted anything so sweet.

Desire muddied his thoughts. If he miscalculated without a

signed contract, she could send him on his way with no chance to redeem himself. When was the last time he'd miscalculated with a woman? When had he known a woman like Juliet Thatcher?

Carrick broke the kiss and pressed her cheek against his chest. To his satisfaction, her heart beat just as fast as his. She would resist him through the summer, eh? It was just as he thought; the men she'd been surrounded with had treated her like one of her mother's whores.

With a final deep breath, he gave her a gentle hug then forced himself to release her. "I shall send a carriage for you in the morning." He nodded at the contract resting next to the deck of cards. "Sign it and join me in Lennoxlove House." He brought her hand to his lips and murmured, "Until we meet again."

Carrick left her there, standing by the table.

CHAPTER 7

Lennoxlove House

The following morning, Carrick's carriage arrived, an extraordinarily large conveyance with elaborate, gilded cherubs and oiled-oak spoke wheels. Liveried footmen tied Juliet's trunk to the back before she stepped inside, the satchel containing the signed contract, clutched close to her breast, and sat down on the plush velvet seat. The carriage jolted, and her heart did a flip as they rolled into motion.

Juliet stared out the window at her mother's townhouse. They'd exchanged farewells the night before, but she glimpsed her mother in the front window. Her mother lifted a hand that clutched a hanky. An expected lump formed in Juliet's throat and she waved in the instant before the carriage left her mother behind. Juliet collapsed back against the cushion. She was being silly. She would see her mother at summer's end, maybe before, if rumors of the duke were true.

A man like him would tire quickly of a woman who didn't

swoon every time he entered a room. Blast it all, she nearly had swooned when she'd kissed him yesterday. What had gotten into her? The devil, that's what. She grimaced. Was Honoria right, did her blood run hot? Nae. It was much worse than that. As much as she wanted to deny it, the man fascinated her.

The days marched by. After six days of travel, the carriage rolled through the market town of Haddington and pulled off the main road onto the long carriageway of the Duke of Hamilton's Scottish estate.

With a growing sense of unease, Juliet eyed the towering pines until they parted and a magnificent castle built of honey-and-pink colored stone slowly came into view. The Hamilton banner snapped in the wind above one stone tower. Picturesque gardens and landscaped lawns rolled past the carriage windows.

The carriage stopped, then tilted to the side. When the footman opened the door, Juliet clasped her satchel and allowed him to hand her out. She descended onto a graveled drive and took a deep breath of the crisp, pine-scented air. The wind soughed through the treetops, reminding her of the dull, distant roar of the ocean.

"Miss Juliet?" a female voice called.

Juliet turned toward the castle's front door where a freckle-faced maid bobbed on the step, urging her forward with a wave of her hand.

"Do hurry, miss." The maid grinned. "The dowager duchess has asked to see you at once."

The dowager duchess?

Juliet hurried to the door and followed the maid through the flagstone entrance and up the wide stairs with their ornate, walnut banisters. Heaven help her, she wasn't sure if she should be relieved or worried that Carrick's mother wanted to see her immediately. The dowager's presence at Lennoxlove would ensure Carrick behaved—she hoped. She'd asked herself a hundred times why he would invite her into the same home he shared with his mother and sister. Did he care that little for convention? He said he would woo her. A tremor rippled through her as it did every time she remembered his words. A man didn't 'woo' his mistress.

She broke from her thoughts when the maid turned into a room to the right.

The sitting room was painted a soft, cheerful yellow and a red-and-gold carpet covered the floor. Afternoon sun flooded the room through large windows that spanned the wall. A young, blonde-haired girl sat in a gold brocade wingback chair, squinting at a book. She glanced up.

"You must be Juliet," a woman's friendly greeting came from the left-hand side of the room.

Juliet whirled as the dowager duchess entered through a second door she hadn't noticed. She was a tall woman in her late fifties with pale blue eyes and blonde hair pulled back in fashionable ringlets only lightly streaked with gray.

"My lady." Juliet dipped into a low curtsey.

"Carrick has been singing your praises, my dear," the woman greeted her kindly as she swept across the room. "My daughter and I are quite excited over the prospect of new gowns. I must say, the dress you're wearing is simply stunning. Is it one of your own?"

Juliet dropped her gaze to her morning dress, a simple enough gown she'd decorated with tastefully elaborate stitching above the waistline. "Why, yes, my lady." She smiled.

"It is gorgeous," the dowager duchess exclaimed. "If your other creations are anything like it, I suspect we will set the pace of fashion. Carrick tells me you just graduated from Lady Peddington's School for Young Ladies."

"That is correct, ma'am," Juliet said.

The dowager gave a business-like nod. "It's heartening to

hear that some of the young ladies of today still value a good education."

Relief surged through Juliet. As she'd hoped, attending Aunt Honey's school had been a wise decision.

"But you can tell us more about that later. You must be tired from your journey." The dowager turned to her daughter and clapped her hands. "Catherine, please show Juliet to her room."

The girl jumped to her feet, obviously delighted to leave her book behind. "Please, follow me." She shot Juliet a wide grin over her shoulder and darted into the hallway.

After bobbing another curtsey, Juliet followed the girl. They walked down the hall and up another flight of stairs.

"This is one of my most favorite rooms," Catherine said as she stopped before an oak-paneled door and opened it.

Juliet entered the bedroom. A fine, gold carpet nearly covered the entire floor. An ornate chest of drawers sat on one wall with a red velvet curtained, four-poster bed on the wall opposite. The room was stunning, but Juliet had eyes only for the view beyond the balcony, visible through the open French doors. With a smile, she dropped her satchel on the bed and hurried to the balcony.

"It's so beautiful." Juliet leaned against the wrought iron rail and drank in the beauty of the gardens, the rolling green woodlands, and the hills beyond. She'd never dreamt she could sleep in so fine a place.

"Aye, beautiful," Carrick's deep voice startled her.

Juliet whirled.

He stood, tall and lean in a white shirt with dark breeches and black leather riding boots. Saints help her, she'd forgotten how handsome he was. Her heart beat a little faster.

"I see you've made the journey safely and in good time." He cocked a brow at his young sister and added, "Catherine, fetch Juliet refreshments, please."

As his sister obligingly skipped through the door, he faced Juliet again.

"I believe you have something for me." His gray eyes twinkled with amusement. "A contract, perhaps?"

The contract. She'd signed and amended the agreement, adding their wager at the bottom. Juliet crossed to her satchel and rummaged through it. Her fingers caught on the soft folds his cravat, the one he'd worn at the Midnight Ball. She smothered a snort and pushed it aside to pull out the folded parchment beneath.

"Only until summer's end," she said, extending the paper toward him.

He strode to her side and took the contract from her. He stood close. Too close. Juliet frowned. The infernal man practically towered over her as he unfolded the paper, scanned its contents and tucked it into his jacket pocket. The corner of his mouth quirked upward.

His smug expression caused her frown to deepen and she crooked a finger to beckon him closer. He angled his head so close that for a moment his heat distracted her, but only for a moment. "I'll never be your mistress."

He tossed his head back and laughed, then dropped a kiss to the top of her ear.

Damn, but his hot breath on her ear made her heart pound.

With a wink, he bowed. "I have pressing business. If you'll excuse me."

Juliet watched his lean hips as he left. She rolled her eyes and picked up her satchel, then pulled out the cravat. Strange how much the little strip of silk had changed her life.

The footmen entered with her trunk and set it where she directed. As soon as they left, she set about unpacking. She'd just pulled out her sewing basket when Catherine returned with a tray of toast, tea, and fruit.

"Why, is that a cravat?" the girl asked after setting the tray down on a small table near the bed.

Juliet glanced over and snagged it from under the girl's outstretched hand. "It's nothing," she quickly assured. "Nothing at all."

Her cheeks heated as she turned and stuffed the cravat into the sewing basket.

Nothing? If it was nothing, then why was she blushing like a fool?

CHAPTER 8

Unforgettable

Never before had a woman gotten so deep under Carrick's skin. That was odd enough, but even stranger, never before had he remembered the details of a woman's face after being away from her for days. But Juliet's? Her features burned in his mind in full, glorious detail, from her dark lashes to the slight worry line between her brows, to the curve of her lips. He couldn't forget her. He had merely to close his eyes and a vision of her gold-streaked hair and laughing blue eyes danced across his mind. At last, she was here, and soon, she'd be his. He strode down the stairs to his mother's sitting room.

"My dear boy." She looked up from a book as he entered. "Sit." She nodded to the chair beside her sofa. "It's time we discussed your marriage."

Marriage? Carrick sat in the indicated chair.

"It's *high* time you wed." She carefully marked the page of the book she'd been reading and set it aside. "I must remind you that you have a duty to the estate."

Carrick stretched out his long legs. He'd heard this so many times before. A maid entered with tea and they remained silent as she set the tray on the table before them, then filled two cups and left.

"I've taken matters into my own hands." His mother lifted her tea cup and sipped.

He tensed. Taken matters into her own hands?

"I've invited a selection of young ladies to a series of dinners this month," she said.

Carrick pushed to his feet. "You are mistaken if you think I will be ambushed by a mob of vapid, title-hungry women." He headed for the door.

"Carrick, wait!" She set her teacup onto its saucer with a clatter.

"There's no need for concern, madam. You will have your grandchild soon enough," he snapped, and left the room.

He paused halfway down the hall. Grandchild? Where had that come from? Damn, his mother picked a fine time to parade women through Lennoxlove House. He didn't have time to concern himself with prospective wives. He had a mistress to seduce.

CHAPTER 9

Made for Pleasure

THE FOLLOWING EVENING, WHEN JULIET OBSERVED, FROM THE sewing room window, the fifth carriage pull up to Lennoxlove House and a beautiful young woman emerge, accompanied by a doting mamma or perhaps an aunt, Juliet realized the Duke of Hamilton was on the hunt for a wife. The question as to why he would contract a mistress while actively seeking a wife arose with the answer hard on its heels: he was a man.

The next morning, the bustle in the kitchen told Juliet that the evening promised more of the same. She steeled herself against the ridiculous disappointment that hovered just below the surface, turned on her heel and headed toward another long day in the sewing room. She slipped down the hallway, reached the Servant stairs, took four steps, then halted. The male laughter coming down the hall was already too familiar: *Carrick.*

She hurried back toward the kitchen, crossed to the larder, and reached the side door seconds later.

"Good morning, ladies."

She froze upon hearing Carrick's voice in the kitchen.

"Has anyone seen Juliet?"

She didn't wait for the staff to inform on her, but hurried out the door and alongside the wall. Her heart pounded. She could go around to the front stairs and enter, then return to her room. Nae, Carrick would find her there in an instant. What could he possibly want with her when he had so many beautiful women vying for his attention?

He's a man, came the answer, yet again.

Juliet glanced at the sky. Grayish clouds skittered across the light blue expanse. It might rain, but not for a bit. She set off east, toward the stables. A morning ride to clear her head was just what she needed. *And Carrick won't find you*, said a small voice. She sighed. This was going to be a long day...and an even longer summer.

When Carrick's laughter filtered up through the window, Juliet paused in threading her needle and peered out the window. There he was again, for the third day in a row, helping another well-dressed lady from her coach in the drive below. The willowy brunette wore an expensive blue silk with an embroidered bodice cut low enough to expose the creamy white mounds of her breasts. Juliet frowned. No wonder he seemed so pleased. With his superior height, the brunette offered quite the view down her bodice. An unexpected pang of jealousy shot through Juliet and she scowled until Carrick passed from view. With a snort of exasperation, she returned to her sewing.

Three days had passed since her arrival at Lennoxlove House. Her stay hadn't been at all what she'd expected. After his initial interest, Carrick had all but vanished from her life. It shouldn't surprise her. After all, she'd predicted that she wouldn't hold his interest. Then there was the parade of women marching through his estate. Redheads, blondes, brunettes. He didn't lack for variety.

The needle pricked her finger. She jerked and dabbed the blood away with a fragment of cut fabric, astonished at the burst of jealousy.

"To work." She bent her head over the yards of peach-colored taffeta destined to become Catherine's finely-stitched gown.

The day passed slowly. The dinner hour arrived and, as the silvery tinkle of a woman's laughter floated up through her window, Juliet decided she'd had enough for the day. It was time to clear her mind, and she couldn't very well do so when a continual symphony of feminine squealing assaulted her ears.

She set aside her sewing and went down the stairs intent on escaping to the quiet of the gardens. The moment she stepped into the cool early evening air, her mood lifted. She took a deep, calming breath. Twilight streaked in dark blues across the sky and a full moon hung low in the east. Ahead, a stone fountain with an immense statue of the Greek god Apollo stood near an inviting stone bench. She stepped onto the garden path, headed toward the fountain, and reached the tall hedges when bootfalls scraped the gravel behind her. Juliet whirled with a gasp as Carrick grasped her shoulder.

"Forgive me," his murmured words sent a thrill down her spine.

The man looked like a Greek god in dark breeches and, heaven help her, no waistcoat. The top two buttons of his startlingly white shirt were undone, and his dark blue cravat hung untied around his neck. Sight of the tanned flesh visible at the open V of his shirt sent a wave of heat racing through her veins.

Mischief lit his eyes. "It's hot," he explained unabashedly, and she realized she was staring—and he'd caught her. He grinned. "Feel free to slip out of your gown, my dear. You'll find the evening air cool on your skin."

Juliet blinked before realizing he was flirting. So, he hadn't lost interest in her, after all. The knowledge pleased her far more than it should. She peered up at him through lowered lashes, prepared to reply, but she froze when he brushed her bottom lip with his thumb and the witty reply vanished.

"You've been hiding," he accused in a gruff voice before letting his hand fall away.

A shriek of laughter emanated from the open dining room windows at the far end of the lawn.

Juliet's temper flared. "How would you know? You've been busy day and *night* with your *guests*."

Carrick's eyes widened in surprise. His lips curved in dry amusement and she realized her mistake.

"I've blundered with my mistress, haven't I?" he asked.

She narrowed her eyes. "I am not—"

"It's my mother's doing, lass," he blithely interrupted, and chucked her under the chin. "She invited a bevy of beauties here in the hopes one might catch my eye. She's determined to see me wed before summer's end."

He was allowing his mother to find him a wife—while his mistress was in residence? Realization struck. He hadn't bedded her, but that didn't matter. She was his mistress. He'd chased her from Edinburgh to London. She hadn't expected sweet words or love. In fact, if he sent her home with the promised money and the cottage as per their agreement, she would be satisfied. But there was something desperately sad about how little she'd come to mean to him in less than a week. She was a fool. She'd never meant anything to him. Why would she? She wasn't a genteel lady like those he entertained.

Juliet pursed her lips. It was just as well she'd decided to become a dressmaker. She clearly made a terrible mistress.

"Forgive my intrusion." She started to step around him.

He stepped sideways and blocked her path. "Aye, I know I'm an incorrigible rogue, lass, but I haven't touched a one of them. Cold fish, the lot."

Why did that please her? But aloud, she pertly replied, "Fish they may be, but they're pedigreed fish."

"I would not have my children born with fins or tails," he said with a vehemence that startled her. "My mother is right, I should have already wed and secured the succession. But, I confess, I believe I should at least *want* to bed my wife."

"One must suffer for the sake of duty," she said dryly.

He heaved a sigh. "Aye, I can only dream of finding pleasure and duty in the same woman."

It was such an outrageous thought for a man of his position that it made her laugh. "I hadn't thought of you as a dreamer."

He quirked a brow. "So, you've been thinking of me?"

The intensity in his gray eyes made her look away. Movement to the right drew her attention.

Carrick seized her arm and pulled her behind the hedges. "That is my mother," he said.

Juliet blanched. "Heavens," she whispered. Alienating the dowager was the last thing she wanted. She pulled free of him and saw that he was staring through the bushes at the figure standing in the open doorway.

"That would explain why she chose now to wage this campaign," he murmured.

"What?" Juliet said.

His features hardened. "Come with me." He grasped her hand.

"I beg your pardon?" She started to yank free, but he entwined his fingers with hers and pulled her around the hedges.

"Are you mad?" To her relief, his mother no longer stood in the doorway. Still, she said, "Your mother will not be pleased to have her dressmaker join the party she's thrown to find you a wife."

"They are sure to gossip over what we were doing in the garden, unchaperoned for an hour or more," he said with a mischievous grin.

Juliet snorted a hearty laugh.

Carrick halted. "My comment was witty, but not to that extent. What is so amusing?"

"An hour?" She couldn't repress a giggle. "You flatter yourself. From what I know of men, the deed takes only minutes."

He tweaked her nose. "Then you are in for a wonderful surprise, sweet."

Juliet rolled her eyes. "Only the old and *infirmed* take that much time."

"Are you calling me impotent?" he asked in an astonished voice.

"I'm calling you uninformed," she answered cheekily.

"Uninformed?"

Carrick locked eyes with her and Juliet realized her mistake. She retreated a step, but he tugged her back. She shook her head. A tiny smile played on his mouth as he drew her closer, inch by inch. She dug her heels in and his smile reached his eyes by the time she reached him.

"Carrick." She intended a reprimand, but his name drifted out as a bare whisper.

His gaze sharpened. He slid an arm around her waist and skimmed the curve of her buttocks until he cupped her derrière. She couldn't tear her eyes from his as he slowly thrust his hips against her. There was no mistaking his erection. He leaned down and her mouth went dry when his warm lips brushed her cheek. He slid moist kisses down her neck. Juliet shivered when he slid his tongue over her collarbone.

Need pulsed at the apex of her thighs. The hand on her buttocks skimmed up her waist, her shoulder, then her neck.

He speared his fingers into the hair bound in a tight chignon. Her heart thundered. He fisted the locks and firmly pulled her head back, baring her neck and—heaven help her—the rise of exposed flesh over her bodice, now warm against evening air that suddenly felt almost cold.

Her pulse quickened in anticipation of his mouth sliding lower. Would he dip his tongue between her bodice and flesh and tease her nipples? God help her, her nipples were so hard they ached.

"I can please you," he murmured against her skin.

Her head reeled. Saints in heaven, if he did nothing more than kiss her breast this instant, she would embarrass herself by screaming his name. She'd never wanted a man like this... never needed his touch. She arched into him.

He gave a low laugh. "Soon, sweet, I promise."

He abruptly stepped back. She stumbled forward. He grasped her arm and steadied her. Juliet looked up at him and frowned.

Carrick lifted a brow. "Uninformed, you say?" With a laugh, he spun and walked away.

JULIET KNEW SHE SHOULD'VE GONE TO BED. THE DOWAGER DIDN'T expect her to work into the night, but she feared where her thoughts would go with nothing to occupy them. Carrick. She now understood his reputation. She also understood his confidence. The man truly was irresistible... Dangerous. He had kissed her once in the days since her arrival and already her resolve had slipped.

Could she last the summer? What if she didn't resist him? Shame rolled over her. She was a normal woman, she experienced desire. That had been long ago, when she was young, long before she'd seen so many men come and go from her mother's brothel. Some were men who loved their wives, but few of them were faithful. Passion simply wasn't worth the lack of trust. She looked up from the hem she was sewing and sought the mantle clock. 9:30. She would finish this hem, then stop for the night. Tomorrow would be another long day.

Footfalls sounded in the hallway outside her door. Juliet looked up as the door opened and Carrick entered, a large basket in hand.

"I knew I'd find you here still working." He stopped in front of her and lifted the basket. "I come bearing gifts." Juliet frowned, and he added, "Supper."

"I've already eaten," she said.

"Bread and cheese, maybe a bit of tea, no doubt." He lifted a brow.

She narrowed her eyes. "You think yourself clever, don't you?"

He grinned. "Aye, I do." He grasped her hand and she had just enough time to set aside the dress as he pulled her to her feet. "Come." He started toward the balcony.

"Carrick, I really must finish this hem before I go to bed."

"Later," he said. They reached the balcony and he opened the doors, then set the basket down and lifted out a plaid blanket. He stepped onto the balcony, shook out the fabric, then laid it on the ground. "Grab the basket and bring it here," he instructed.

With a sigh, Juliet picked up the basket and carried it onto the balcony. Clouds drifted slowly across a sky littered with stars. She had to admit, it was a beautiful night. Carrick clasped her hand and steadied her as she sank onto the plaid, then he sat beside her and lifted from the basket a bottle of wine, a wrapped cloth, which he opened to reveal blueberry pastries, and a plate with a cloth over it, which held cold chicken. Cheese, of course, along with two plates, two glasses and silverware.

"This is a feast," she said.

"A feast for two," he said.

"What about your guests?" she said.

He shook his head. "They are far too busy admiring each other's dresses and hairstyles to miss me."

She knew that was untrue, but couldn't help a grimace. "You have my sympathies."

He laughed, then filled a plate, which he passed to her. He then poured wine in both glasses before filling his own plate.

Juliet took her first bite. "This chicken is quite good."

"Mrs. Allenby is an excellent cook," he replied, taking a hearty gulp of wine. "What are you sewing?"

"A day dress for your mother. She already had the fabric. A beautiful canary yellow muslin."

"Yellow is her favorite color," he said.

Surprised to find herself so hungry, Juliet set about eating her chicken and washing it down with the wine.

"How did your mother take it when you left?" Carrick asked.

Juliet shot him a dry look. "She was very pleased, as you must know. You paid her a handsome sum."

He gave a small smile. "She is a skilled negotiator."

"It is not the first time she sold me."

He looked sharply at her. "She told me you were…"

Juliet lifted a brow. "A virgin?" Anger stabbed. "I see. You want a virgin to deflower." Why hadn't it occurred to her?

He shook his head. "Nae, I did not—" He paused. "The contract had nothing to do with whether or not you were a virgin. Your mother said you were untouched. I am simply surprised she lied."

"People lie all the time." Juliet regarded him. "If you feel you were cheated, I will return home and ask nothing further from you."

He stared for a moment, then a slow smile spread across his

face. "I have until summer's end to seduce you. That's what I intend to do."

"Even if I am *used property?*"

His smile vanished. "You are not *property*. Is that what you believe I think of you?"

He was genuinely offended. "No," she answered softly.

He stared for another heartbeat as if uncertain, then said, "I would have made the same offer to your mother whether I thought you were virgin or not." His gaze intensified. "I want you to know that."

A tiny bit of guilt stabbed, but only a tiny bit. "Well, my mother did not lie."

He blinked. "Then you lied?"

"No. I only said my mother had sold me once before. I never said I got...used."

"You allowed me to believe you had lost your virginity."

She shrugged. "Sometimes people simply leave something out."

He threw his head back and laughed. "I can see, I'm going to have to tread very carefully with you."

Juliet nodded as she finished her chicken. "We dressmakers are a hearty breed."

His eyes lit with mischief. "I shall take great care, then." He reached into the basket, pulled out a small, smooth wooden box and handed it to her.

Juliet looked at him. "What is it?"

He nodded at the box. "Open it and find out."

She hesitated, then took it. Juliet cast a curious glance at him, then lifted the box lid. Inside, on black velvet, rested a silver locket with a silver chain. She frowned. "I don't understand."

"It's a gift."

"But why?"

"Ladies do not ask a gentleman why they give them gifts," he said.

She stiffened. "I see."

"I doubt you do, lass. I have no ulterior motive. I thought you might like it, that's all. Look inside the locket."

She was tempted not to accept it, but setting the box aside, she lifted the locket and opened the clasp. She gasped. An intricate miniature of her mother filled the right side. Juliet snapped her gaze onto Carrick. "I-I don't understand."

"Do you like it?" he asked.

She looked back at the miniature and nodded.

"That's why I did it."

Tears burned the corners of her eyes. She swiped at a teardrop that broke through her resolve and ran a finger over the small portrait. "It's beautiful." She looked at him. "Thank you."

He smiled, the pleasure reaching to his eyes, and her heart tugged. Oh, this man was dangerous, very, very dangerous. Despite the admonition, she leaned across the food and pressed a kiss to his cheek. He went very still.

She withdrew and shook her head. "What made you think of this? It's not as if I will be away from my mother all that long."

He shrugged. "A daughter needn't be separated from her mother very long to miss her."

Juliet's heart pounded. "I had better finish the hem on the dress."

He nodded, pushed to his feet, and extended a hand. As she placed her hand in his, his fingers closed around hers with such gentleness that the tears threatened again. She would never be one of the fine ladies he chose as his wife. He pulled her to her feet and tugged her into his arms and with a slow grin, bent and covered her mouth with his. She should have pushed him away, should have reminded him that she would never become his mistress, but instead, she found herself melting against him, breathing of him deeply as his tongue slipped past her lips. She lost track of time as their tongues sparred, and when he drew back, for an instant, her surroundings seemed to spin.

He steadied her. "Are you all right, lass?"

She nodded, but the satisfied smile she glimpsed in the instant before he turned away told her he was well aware that he'd touched her heart.

~

JULIET TOSSED AND TURNED INTO THE WEE HOURS OF THE NIGHT. Carrick had played her like an instrument. For hours, she'd lain on her bed, aching with need.

As the moon rose high in the sky outside her window, she gave up all pretense of sleep, threw her shawl over her shoulders and slipped from her room. Mrs. Allenby made a very nice lemon water, perhaps it would help.

She'd gone scarcely more than a yard from her door when Carrick's soft voice drifted through the darkness, "Why are you wandering in the night like a wraith, Juliet?"

She spun, then froze at sight of his silhouette leaning against the opposite wall.

"I can't sleep," she whispered.

"Then do not try, lass." He started toward her.

CHAPTER 10

Mistress

CARRICK REACHED JULIET AND CAUGHT HER CLOSE. HE HAD nearly knocked on her bedroom door a dozen times, unsure if she were truly ready for him. But the way she melted against him, he knew beyond a doubt that she wanted him. With a growl, he swept her into his arms and entered her bedchamber, then pushed the door closed with a kick.

Bright moonlight bathed the room in a soft, silvery glow. Carrick set her feet on the carpet and pulled the shawl from her shoulders, letting the moon's light illuminate the outline of her soft curves. Her hair fell over her slim shoulders. She was so beautiful he could scarcely breathe.

He covered her mouth with his. She gasped. He urged her back toward the bed. Without prompting, she parted her lips and he swept inside. Their tongues met in a tingling caress. He sucked her tongue into his mouth. She leaned into him and anticipation thrummed through him.

His knee bumped the bed and she jarred. Carrick lowered her onto the mattress and came down on top of her. She drew a deep breath. Her nipples poked through the thin fabric of her shift. She wanted him. Carrick took one hardened nipple into his mouth and sucked through the cloth of her shift. Juliet grasped his shoulders and arched into his mouth. She slid one hand up his arm, his neck, then threaded her fingers into his hair. He needed her naked. He needed her cool fingers around his shaft. First... He shifted to the other nipple. Her fingers tightened in his hair.

He grunted. "I know, love."

Carrick released the nipple, then shoved to his knees and pulled her upright with him.

She gasped, "Are we finished already?"

He gave a strangled laugh. "Not by half." He grasped the hem of her shift, then pulled it up and over her head.

His breath caught. Moonlight bathed her creamy skin in a glow that gave her an almost ethereal quality. She was a goddess and he planned to worship every inch of her.

He tossed the shift to the floor.

"It's not fair," she said.

He started from the trance. "What?"

"It's not fair."

Carrick frowned. "What isn't fair? I have only just begun—"

"I'm naked. You're not."

His heart thundered. Christ Almighty, she was a brazen lass.

"I cannot argue with a lady," he said.

She tilted her head. "I am no lady, sir."

He gave his head a single shake. "Nae, you are a goddess."

Her mouth quirked. Carrick couldn't believe it. She was amused. He would change that. He jumped to his feet, immensely glad he'd removed his boots earlier. Then, heedless of the buttons, he yanked his shirt open. He sluffed the shirt from his shoulders, yanked open the buttons on his breeches, then shoved them down his hips.

Her audible gasp caused his cock to pulse. No other woman had ever affected him like this. Carrick kicked the breeches aside, then crawled onto the bed and eased her onto her back, then straddled her. She stared up at him, her features in shadow. He glanced at the night table and considered lighting a candle. He wanted to see her. Could he wait the moment it would take to light the damn thing?

She lifted a hand and he froze when she wrapped her arm around his neck and drew him closer. Apparently, *she* couldn't wait.

"You're so beautiful," he whispered in the instant before their lips met.

He settled his body on top of hers. His cock brushed the curve of her abdomen. This time, she sucked his tongue into her mouth. He sparred with her, and covered a breast with one hand. She arched, and her hard nipple pressed his palm. Dare he... Carrick lightly pinched the nipple. She drew a sharp breath. The sound heated his blood.

He broke the kiss, then lowered his mouth to her left breast and flicked the right nipple while he lightly pinched the other nipple again.

She seized his shoulders. Her desperate grip sent a wave of desire through him. Slowly, he thrust his member against her belly. Sweet discomfort tightened his bollocks. He needed to be inside her. But not yet. He had to show her that what existed between them was nothing like the quick encounters that took place in her mother's brothel.

Carrick placed soft kisses on her breasts, then her neck, then her mouth again. She drew in a shuddering breath. When he reached between them and brushed his fingers along the curls between her legs, she tensed. He kissed her again, gently and slipped a finger between her folds. Blood roared through his ears. She was so wet. He forced patience and slowly slid a finger inside her.

Juliet stilled, and he hid a smile. The woman of the world was not quite prepared for the realities of a man stroking her pleasure point. With his thumb, he messaged her swollen nub as he slowly thrust a finger in and out of her channel. To his delight, she began to move her hips in rhythm with his strokes. By God, the woman was hot blooded. He licked her nipple.

"Carrick," she moaned.

Hearing her call his name sent a wave of unexpected satisfaction through him. She began to move faster. He kept his rhythm even. Her fingers dug into his shoulders. Moonlight splashed across her face, bathing her skin in an ethereal glow. His cock strained so hard against his skin he thought the damned member would break free and plunge inside her of its own accord.

Juliet abruptly stiffened and cried out. Her channel milked his finger. Carrick yanked his finger from her channel, closed his mouth over her sex and sucked.

"God have mercy," she cried, and pulsed beneath his tongue as a second climax rolled over her.

She drew a shuddered breath. Carrick pushed upright and quickly fitted his cock to her opening. Her tight opening closed around the sensitive crown. The need to drive into her nearly drove him out of his mind. He slid a hand beneath her buttocks and locked his gaze on her face. He couldn't read her expression.

"Do you trust me?" he asked.

She grasped his arm and said in a barely audible whisper, "Yes."

"This will hurt for only an instant," he said, and thrust into her hilt deep.

She stiffened. Carrick froze until Juliet released a breath and relaxed. He lowered his weight onto her, wrapped his arms around her and buried his face in her hair as he began to move inside her. He was ashamed to admit he wouldn't last long with her magnificent heat wrapped so tightly around him. He tried to think about the accounts he would have to deal with first thing in the morning, but she lifted her hips to meet his thrusts and his climax rolled over him without warning. Intense pleasure ripped through him and, with a startled cry, he spilled his seed inside her.

Heart racing, he continued to drive into her half a dozen times as he milked the last vestiges of pleasure from his member. At last, he collapsed onto her slender form for several heartbeats, then slid off her. He pulled her close.

"I can do better, I promise. Give me ten minutes, and I'll prove myself."

He felt her smile against his chest. She was laughing at him again. He really had to do something about that. He gently pushed her onto her back and looked at her with wonder.

"You were incredible," he whispered.

He kissed her again, tenderly.

The wind rustled through the open window, blowing her hair across his bare chest. He wanted to take her again, but knew her tender flesh needed to rest. He'd have to wait. Instead, he drew her further up into the pillows, and cradled her in his arms. She heaved a sigh and closed her eyes.

His mistress. Aye, she was his mistress. At last.

He lay on his back and closed his eyes, just for a moment.

CARRICK AWOKE AS THE FIRST RAYS OF SUN FILTERED THROUGH the window, his cock hard with the memory of last night and a new, strange need that coursed through him. He turned on his side, facing the slight form in the bed next to him and his heartbeat quickened. The sheet had slipped down the rise of her breasts and he glimpsed the edges of the soft pink areolas he'd tasted last night. Her hair, a sensuous tangle of thick locks, framed her face and lay across one full breast. His cock pulsed. He grinned. She was truly and fully his mistress.

Juliet arched and stretched. He dropped a kiss to her throat, then added a soft series of kisses under the line of her jaw. She tensed, then relaxed under the ministrations of his tongue and moaned that same husky sound that had driven him wild last night. Shivers raced down his spine.

"I need you." He grasped her hand and wrapped her fingers around his shaft. "Now."

He gently thrust against her loose fist. To his surprise, she pulled away and pushed him flat on his back, his cock jutting up like a pillar of marble. Juliet lowered her lashes, then swung her slim leg over his hips and poised her entrance above his erection.

"Ride me, lass." He grasped her hips and tensed in readiness for her channel to sheath him.

"So demanding," Juliet teased as she took the tip of his throbbing manhood into her slim body.

She tortured him. Horribly. Repeatedly sliding down an inch before lifting herself off until, at last, he could bear it no longer and he shoved her down onto his hard length as he thrust upward. She gasped and tossed her head back in delight. With her heat fully encasing him, he began to rock. They were meant for each other. He couldn't control himself. Not with the way she moved. Within minutes, her lashes fluttered as she shuddered in ecstasy and he came with a loud groan, pumping himself into her until he'd milked his cock to the very last.

When he finished, he lifted her off him and she lay her head on his chest as he traced the length of her spine with a fingertip.

Neither spoke for a time. It wasn't until the distant chime of the grandfather clock announced the breakfast hour that Juliet bolted upright. "Heavens! I'm late to fit your sister's gown."

Amused, he watched her dive from the bed and dart to the armoire.

"Don't bother with the under drawers," he said. "You won't need them."

She snorted and stuffed her arms through her dress sleeves, then shimmied the dress down over lush breasts. His cock twitched. She would be spending an inordinate amount of time on her back with him between her legs.

At the door, she paused and looked over her shoulder.

"We'll continue this later, lass." He rose. Her eyes flicked to his erection before she turned and left.

Carrick caught sight of her drawers on the floor. He grinned. It was going to be a good day.

CHAPTER 11

Blind Man's Bluff

NEVER IN HER WILDEST DREAMS HAD JULIET THOUGHT THAT bedding a man could be so…consuming. She could still feel the heat of Carrick's body on hers and the warmth of his breath in her hair as he'd groaned her name.

"What made you decide to become a dressmaker?" Catherine asked Juliet.

Juliet started from her thoughts. She pushed the needle through the sky-blue velvet. She sat in the drawing room's bay window as Catherine lounged on a nearby settee, perusing swatches of lace.

"We must all do something. I like creating clothes and I am —I hope—skilled at it."

"Indeed, you are, my dear." The dowager turned a page in the book she was reading.

"I don't like sewing at all," Catherine said. "I know that's a terrible thing to say. Young ladies are supposed to like sewing. But I don't."

"Well, fortunately, you don't need to love it to be skilled at darning a pair of socks or repairing a hem," Juliet said.

"You see there, Catherine, the dowager said, "Juliet understands that sewing is a skill that a lady must have."

"I don't think that's what she said, Mama. She is only saying that just because I don't like it, doesn't mean I can't do it."

Juliet hid a smile.

"What else do you do besides sew?" Catherine said.

"I read, of course. I paint a little, and I speak a little Latin and French."

Catherine made a face. "Surely, you do other things that are much more fun than that?"

"I like to read," Juliet said. "Have you found any lace you like yet?"

She shrugged. "Carrick said you live in London. I adore London. When last we were there, Carrick took me riding in the park every day. Do you go riding in the park as well? Carrick has a wonderful phaeton. I wish that I could drive it, but he says ladies don't do such things."

"He's quite right, of course," Juliet said, and she glimpsed the approving glance the dowager sent her way.

Catherine must've seen it, as well, for she said, "You're only agreeing because Mama is here. But I think you know that a lady is just as capable of driving a phaeton as a man is."

"One must be very skilled to drive any kind of carriage," Juliet said in all seriousness.

"I feel certain I could learn," Catherine said, but Juliet knew better than to say yay or nae.

"Where in London do you live?" Catherine asked. "We will have to visit you when next we are there. Isn't that right, Mama?"

"Indeed, it is," the dowager agreed.

Juliet's pulse quickened, but she had practiced a thousand times what she would say to the first person who asked her address in London, and she rattled off the address of the home of Bonnie Macmillan's milliner shop, which she would rent when she returned to London.

"I'm so glad we were able to come to Lennexlove House to be with you," Catherine said.

Juliet smiled. "I am glad, too."

"It was fortunate we hadn't yet left for London when Carrick told us he was bringing you."

Juliet looked at her sharply. They weren't in Lennexlove House when Carrick said he would bring her here? She had assumed they were already in residence. It had to mean he'd planned on bringing her here alone, and had only brought them later when he'd realized she expected them there.

Suddenly, Juliet felt the dowager's eyes on her. Her fingers trembled. Did the woman suspect what had happened between her and Carrick last night? She would not be pleased. She might even demand Carrick send her away. Strangely, though she'd wanted to be sent away, the idea of leaving now depressed her.

A knock on the door made Juliet jump, and a maid entered and curtsied, but to Juliet's surprise, the maid faced her instead of the dowager.

"His Grace wishes to see you in the library," the maid announced. "At once."

Juliet felt her face flush. "Are you certain?" she asked in a steady voice.

"Aye, Miss," the maid replied. "He came looking for ye in the kitchen. Mrs. Allenby sent me to find you."

Juliet's heart thundered. How could she explain his summons? She didn't dare look at the dowager.

"I imagine he received the bill for the fabrics we ordered," Catherine said with a laugh.

Juliet could have kissed her. She wasn't certain it would be the dressmaker the master of the house would take to task for overspending on fabric, but the excuse was far better than the blank stare she knew she wore.

"Perhaps I overdid it," she murmured as she rose to her feet, keenly aware of the dowager's sharp eyes latching onto her. "Put the swatch you like best here." Juliet patted her sewing basket, smoothed her skirts, then left the room.

She hurried down the hallway. She would have his hide for this. What had gotten into him, summoning her like...like she was his mistress?

Juliet arrived to find the library door ajar and peeked inside. It was an impressive room, painted a warm shade of yellow. Its windows overlooked the sprawling lawn and gardens. Tall, rosewood bookcases lined the walls and the smell of wood polish and leather permeated the air. Juliet eased the door open and caught sight of Carrick at his desk, penning a letter. Her breath caught. His sleeves were rolled up to reveal tanned forearms. A lock of hair had fallen across his forehead. He glanced up and a smile lit his face.

"You sent for me?" Juliet entered and closed the door behind her as he set down his pen and leaned back in his chair.

He lifted an eyebrow and she knew he was wondering why she'd closed the door. Let him wonder. She took three paces to his desk then stopped. "Have you lost your mind, Carrick?"

He blinked.

"I was with your mother and sister when the maid arrived to inform me that you'd summoned me."

His eyes widened slightly, then he gave a lopsided grin that caused her stomach to flip. "I didn't find you in the sewing room or the kitchen and assumed you were avoiding me." He shrugged. "I decided one of the maids would have better luck finding you."

Juliet stared. He looked so contrite and so...so damnably

attractive that she suddenly wondered how she was going to escape this—him—unscathed. She wasn't, she realized. She'd already lost the bet. He owned her for the next year. How long could she continue as the dowager's dressmaker before the older woman figured out the truth?

His eyes darkened and suddenly his mother, their bet, nothing else mattered. "Come closer, my dear. You know where you belong."

"Where do I belong?" she whispered.

He smiled. "In my arms."

Her pulse quickened. Juliet stepped around the desk, but stopped beyond reach. He leaned forward, seized her arm, and tugged her into his lap. She shrieked. He laughed and hugged her close while she twisted in a halfhearted attempt at freedom. Her hip bumped his hard length and she froze.

"Good Lord, Carrick. I'm surprised you have any energy left after last night."

He laughed and hugged her tighter. "I told you I would have many wonderful surprises for you."

Her heart began to pound, and she realized she wanted him so badly it hurt. Juliet pushed away from him and he released her as she slid from his lap. With a quick twitch of her skirt, she knelt before him. His gaze sharpened when she reached for the buttons on his breeches and slowly unfastened them. Her fingers brushed the bulge straining against the constraints and he sucked in a startled breath. Embarrassment warmed her cheeks when her fingers trembled slightly as she freed the last button. His erection spring free and his shirt tented. She pushed aside the shirt and heat rushed through her at sight of his rigid manhood. She raised her gown to her thighs and straddled his thighs.

He closed his eyes and took a long, luxurious breath as she slowly slid down onto his hard length. With a sigh of pleasure, she dropped her gown, the silk making a soft swish as it covered them both.

He skimmed his fingers lightly over her arms and tugged her bodice until her breasts spilled over the neckline. Eager to feel his mouth on her flesh, she arched forward and pulled his face toward her. He sucked a nipple into his mouth.

She shivered. "Carrick," she whispered.

Slowly, she lifted off him, then lowered until he filled her. She rose, and he thrust to meet her downward motion. Pain and pleasure spiked. Juliet braced her hands on his shoulders, steadying her torso so that he could continue to suck her breasts as she rode him. He grasped her hips and brought her down hard. Her breath caught. The man knew how to please a woman.

He increased their rhythm and suckled her other breast. Pleasure built inside her core. Her nipple slipped from his mouth and his grasp on her hips tightened as she slammed down on him. His jaw tensed. A wave of gratification rolled over her. She pleased him. Her climax caught her off guard. Juliet threw her head back and arched. He rammed his cock deeper. She cried out and light flashed behind her eyes. It seemed the world spun around her. Her body went weak as a kitten.

Juliet was vaguely aware of his groan as he ground himself against her sex. She'd seen the girls in her mother's brothel backed against walls while their customers pumped into them, had heard more stories than she could remember of the mechanics of the joining of a man and woman. But she'd never heard the girls speak of this sort of...magic. Is that what it was, magic?

Juliet collapsed onto his chest and listened to the powerful thump of his heart until its rhythm slowed.

Carrick buried his face in her hair. "I can't get enough of

you." He nuzzled her neck. "Come to my bed. Let's spend the day there."

Juliet snorted and reluctantly straightened. "You know very well I have gowns to sew."

"As if my mother and sister don't have enough of the blasted things." He ran his hands over her breasts and tweaked her nipples.

She shivered.

"Come to my bed," he repeated.

Juliet pulled her sleeves back over her shoulders and slid off his lap. He tucked his shirt back in his pants, then fastened his pants and released a long breath.

"I imagine your mother and sister are still in the drawing room where I left them." A thread of panic wound through her. "Lord, the dowager will wonder why I took so long."

He grasped her hand and his expression sobered. "I will deal with my mother."

The panic intensified. "Carrick, she can't know—"

A knock sounded at the door. "Carrick," his mother called.

Juliet yanked her gaze onto the door. Dear God, if the dowager saw her before she has a chance to smooth every hair back into place.

The door knob started to turn, and Juliet dropped to her knees.

"What the—" Carrick began, but she scurried under his desk as the door opened. She pulled her knees to her chest. He turned, and she was forced sideways against the wood when his knees nearly struck her shoulder. He shifted, and Juliet realized he was looking up from his desk. His arms rested on the desktop. Dear God, she hoped his expression gave away nothing of the fact that his mistress was hiding there.

"I thought I would find Juliet here," the dowager's voice came from the direction of the door.

Juliet jammed her eyes closed and silently prayed, *Please, please, please, do not come in.*

"You missed her," he replied.

The door creaked, and Juliet's heart thundered. Was the dowager entering the room and closing the door behind her or had she left?

"I am busy, Mother," Carrick said, and Juliet's heart fell. The dowager hadn't left

"I have planned another dinner for tonight," she said.

"I believe you told me that." His right arm shifted slightly, and Juliet thought he might be writing as he had been when she arrived.

"Catherine and I will be spending the autumn and winter in Edinburgh."

"That is your habit," he replied distractedly.

"Lady Audrey is very nice, don't you agree?" The dowager's voice was closer. Silk rustled, and Juliet realized she was sitting in the chair opposite Carrick's desk.

"I'm too busy to discuss women, Mother," he said.

"Even Juliet?"

He jerked.

Juliet tensed.

"I beg your pardon?" he said.

"I'm no fool, Carrick," his mother said. "I know —

He shoved his chair back and stood. "I will thank you to keep anything you *know* to yourself, madam."

He turned, and his legs disappeared from sight as he strode around the desk. Juliet could barely hear his bootfalls through the pounding of her heart in her ears. The doorknob rattled, then he said, "I am busy, Mother."

Three heartbeats later, the dowager said, "Lady Audrey will be attending the dinner tonight." Her voice was farther away.

"How kind of you to invite her a second time," Carrick replied in a cold voice.

"I have never known you to act like this," the dowager said.

"You have never gone so far as to choose my bride for me," he said.

A moment of silence passed. "It is time you married, Carrick. Whatever pleasures you might seek—"

"Madam, I have been patient thus far."

The warning in his voice sent a shiver down Juliet's back.

"Then I will see you at dinner," the dowager said.

The door clicked shut and a moment later, Carrick's legs came back into view. He squatted and bent his head so that he could make eye contact. "Come on out, love."

Juliet pulled her dress to her knees and crawled from beneath the desk. He grasped her hand and pulled her to her feet.

"She's right, you know," Juliet said as she brushed imaginary dust off her dress. She gave thanks that her voice remained steady.

He placed a finger beneath her chin and she froze when he tilted her face toward his. "Never mind my mother."

How could she possibly do that? The woman was determined to see her son wed. "She's your mother," Juliet whispered.

"And she has nothing to do with us," he replied.

Juliet stepped away. "I'd better return to the drawing room." She started to turn, but he grabbed her arm.

"Not that way." He tugged her to the bookshelves near the sideboard and pressed on a shelf. It sprang away from the wall.

"What in the world?" she exclaimed.

He grinned. "Lennoxlove is full of surprises." The look in his eyes said that he, too, was full of surprises.

~

JULIET SPENT THE AFTERNOON IN THE SEWING ROOM TRYING HER

best to ignore thoughts of Carrick. Carrick laughing. Carrick staring down at her. Carrick caressing her breasts. Carrick in another woman's arms. Why did it bother her so? She knew the proper place of a mistress—in practice, anyway. In reality, remembering her place was so much harder.

As evening approached, the crunch of wheels on the graveled drive drew her attention to the window, yet again. Despite the conviction to ignore everything outside her room, she shifted and looked out the window. Her heart wrenched when Carrick stepped into view as a carriage rolled to a stop in front of the house. He opened the carriage door and took the elegant hand that reached toward him. The dark-haired beauty wore an olive-green velvet dress as fine as any Juliet had ever seen. She gave a silvery laugh that reached the window.

The woman slipped her hand into the crook of his arm and Juliet glimpsed his smile as he turned toward the house. Her heart squeezed. He was charming. They disappeared from view and his baritone laugh abruptly cut off when the door shut. The evening was young. Who knew how many more young ladies would arrive?

Juliet reached into her sewing basket to pull out a spool of thread, but her fingers caught on the silky folds of Carrick's cravat. Slowly, she withdrew the narrow length of fabric and pressed it against her cheek. Incredibly, it still carried his scent. Spicy sandalwood.

The young woman's silvery laugh came again in the distance.

Juliet stiffened and suddenly felt rather foolish to be sniffing the cravat like a loyal hound. She stuffed it back into the basket. She wasn't about to sit there, listening to the sounds of their merrymaking, not when she could sit in the quieter solitude of the servant quarters one floor up. Quickly, she gathered her sewing and went upstairs.

The evening dragged. Her thoughts returned too often to

the memory of Carrick's lips on her skin—and his smile for the beautiful dark-haired lady. Just *how* did he entertain the debutantes in the drawing room below? When the clock struck ten, her mind still churned with uncomfortable questions. She set her sewing aside and stretched her stiff neck. Her fingers ached. The day was done, but the guests remained. Were they staying for a house party? She nibbled her lip. While she yearned to slip into Carrick's bed, she refused to consider such an action while he entertained other women.

"It's a book for you tonight, Juliet," she muttered. Perhaps for many nights to come—if she were wise. A book was a poor substitute for Carrick's lips, but it was the best—and safest— her evening could offer.

After a quick detour to the kitchen for a simple meal of fresh bread and cheese, she hurried down the hall toward the library. The candles and oil lamps burned low in their sconces and wall holders. In the drawing room, just three doors away, someone played the pianoforte.

At the hum of voices, Juliet quickened her steps to the library then stopped outside its door when feminine laughter drifted toward her. She recognized too well the titter of a woman trying to impress a man. Which one of them was laughing? She crept toward the drawing room. If she was careful, no one would notice if she stole a peek.

Catherine suddenly darted into the hall.

Juliet stopped short and pivoted on her heel.

"Juliet," Catherine called, but Juliet hurried away. An instant later, Catherine reached her side and caught her hand. "Oh, do play with us, Juliet." The young girl giggled. *"Please,* Juliet!"

"I really shouldn't." Juliet tried to shake free.

"Don't be a ninny." Catherine tugged her several paces toward the drawing room. "Come join the fun."

Juliet knew she should break free—for a mistress didn't socialize with ladies invited to respectable parties. Her mother had pounded that into her head long before she truly understood what the words meant.

They reached the drawing room. Juliet took two paces into the room, caught sight of Carrick and stopped. The Duke of Hamilton stood before the fire, dressed in black breeches with a gray brocade waistcoat, white shirt, and a fine red silk, elaborately tied cravat. He smiled as he examined a large sapphire ring against the firelight. Half a dozen guests gathered around him, three of whom were ladies vying for the closest position.

"It's such a beautiful ring, Carrick," a petite redhead in an expensive blue satin evening gown said. "A truly stunning ring any woman would be *pleased* to wear."

"Not just *any* woman." The dowager shifted in the nearby settee. Her voice held a distinct note of pride. "Hamilton brides have worn that ring for the past eighty years."

Brides. Juliet turned to leave.

Catherine shut the door, her back to the wood, and grinned. "Juliet's come to play with us."

All eyes turned onto her.

"Ah, Juliet," the dowager said.

Juliet faced the older woman, careful to keep her gaze from straying to Carrick.

The older woman waved her forward. "Come, join us."

Juliet hesitated. If the woman disapproved of her presence, it was difficult to tell. Juliet needn't glance at the prospective brides to know they didn't approve. She felt their assessing gazes inventory her face, figure and, no doubt, her clothes. A sliver of satisfaction bolstered her. In that regard, they would not find her lacking.

Catherine bounced over to her brother. "We have more than enough players now."

Juliet couldn't halt her gaze from following the girl.

Catherine tugged his sleeve. "Juliet's here for a game of Blind Man's Bluff."

Carrick grinned down at his sister. "Then what are we waiting for?" His attention shifted to Juliet.

Other guests laughed and rose from their seats as Carrick started toward her. She should leave. She knew it. Yet, her feet wouldn't move.

He reached her side. "Good evening, Miss Thatcher." He bowed and peered down at her with a twinkle in his gray eyes.

An answering smile curled her lips and she curtseyed low. "Good evening to you, as well," she murmured, deliberately refusing to utter the expected words 'my lord' or 'your grace'. Indeed, she wouldn't join the gaggle of fawning creatures in the room.

A sharp clapping of hands startled them both and Juliet blinked to find the dowager watching them closely.

"Let the game begin." She clapped her hands a few more times and raised her brow in an obvious reprimand.

Juliet averted her gaze, and wished mightily that she had left. Carrick chuckled, looped his arm through hers and drew her toward the circle of players.

"Allow me to go first," a slim gentleman with thinning brown hair offered.

Catherine obligingly tied the band of cloth over his eyes and spun him around as the countdown began. The players fanned out across the room and began calling his name.

Juliet edged toward the door.

"Edward, this way," the calls began as the man began to bump about the drawing room, arms outstretched.

Juliet retreated another pace and Carrick edged closer. He leaned down, clearly intending to whisper in her ear, when the redheaded woman bumped his arm.

"Forgive me, Your Grace." She giggled and lay her hand on his arm.

Carrick's expression hardened, and Juliet's heart sang.

The blindfolded man stumbled past two women who sidestepped him, and he collided with Carrick. The man seized Carrick's cravat and announced, "It's Hamilton."

Carrick snorted a laugh. "Damn cravat," he said in a low voice, and glanced sideways at Juliet. He faced the thin man. "I'll take this, my dear fellow." Carrick whipped the blindfold off him and began tying it over his eyes.

Catherine appeared at his side and began to spin her brother in circles. The redheaded woman giggled and made no move to fan out and join the others.

Catherine rolled her eyes in disgust. "Let's change up the rules, shall we? The *last* one Carrick catches will earn a kiss."

Above the blindfold, Carrick's brows knit into a frown.

A chorus of 'ohhs' went up amongst the woman and the redhead said, "How delightful," then darted away.

"I say, I don't care for this new rule," the thin gentleman objected.

Carrick cocked his head to the side and teased. "Then, Edwards, here I come."

As he took a step forward, one of the women pushed Juliet into his path. He caught her arm and tensed, then relaxed and slid his fingers down to her wrists to give her a little yank. She stumbled and fell against his chest.

Catherine clapped. "I changed my mind. I say Carrick must kiss the first woman he catches."

Juliet stiffened. The other women protested loudly.

"That isn't fair."

"That will teach you not to push other players, Lady Audrey," Catherine said.

Carrick planted a chaste kiss on Juliet's forehead. "'Tis Miss Thatcher," he said with conviction.

"Bravo!" Edwards laughed.

"Enough of this game." Carrick tore off the blindfold.

"Let us sing, shall we?" Catherine suggested as she skipped to the pianoforte.

"It's getting late, Catherine dear," the dowager objected.

Her daughter ignored her and plopped down at the pianoforte, then began to play. As the room filled with voices—and the women swooped over to commandeer Carrick's attention—Juliet made good her escape. She ducked into the library and turned to close the door when Carrick stepped inside. Juliet cried out when he caught her in his arms.

"Where are you running as if the devil himself were after you?"

"To my room," she said, and silently added, where I belong. "You should return to your guests."

He peered down at her, looking more handsome than a man had a right to, with his lips curled into a lazy smile. "Let them wonder. I've had enough of duty tonight."

The words made her heart thud, but then her attention caught on the word 'duty.' Duty would always stand between them. The thought soured her mood.

He drew his brows into a faint, puzzled line. "What is it?"

"Nothing," she lied.

"I'm no fool, Juliet. What's bothering you?"

"It's nothing, truly." She shook her head. "You shouldn't ignore your guests in favor of your mistress."

Surprise overcame his puzzlement, then the gray eyes staring down at her glittered. "Make no mistake, Juliet, a paper doesn't dictate what lies between us. I would tear it in half this moment, if not for the fact that it secures your wellbeing."

There was truth to that, no matter how hard it was to admit. Already, she'd earned her house and yearly sum. She winced. She'd fallen prey to his charms so fast. Damn her passionate blood.

"My mother will be pleased." She couldn't hide the bitterness in her voice.

He grasped her shoulder. "Forget your mother and that damn contract. What *we* feel is the only thing that matters." He drew her close once again and softly traced the outline her jaw. "You're mine and mine alone," he whispered. *"My* mistress."

My mistress. The way he said the words made her feel like a cherished possession, and the gentleness of his touch sent shivers down her spine. He dropped his head to nuzzle her temple and she melted against him, keenly aware of the rise and fall of his chest as he inhaled deeply before he pressed his forehead against hers.

"I can't get you out of my thoughts." He pulled back enough to look in her eyes. "You're not like any woman I've known."

Juliet searched the depths of his gray eyes. "I most certainly have never met a man like you."

He held her closer. Then kissed her. The passionate ravage of her mouth softened to an intimate nibble. The thud of his heart beat in time with hers. She'd thought him all fire and passion, but this tender, gentle exchange left her weak-kneed with desire. Might she—

A sharp knock on the door caused her to jerk back.

The dowager's muffled voice called from the other side, "Carrick? Are you in there?"

Carrick's head jerked in the direction of the door.

"Carrick?" the dowager repeated.

The door knob rattled and Juliet broke free of his embrace.

"Juliet, wait," Carrick hissed.

He grabbed for her, but she bolted toward the servants' door. She couldn't face the dowager. Juliet winced and dashed up the stairs.

At last, she slipped into her room. She flopped onto her back on the bed and contemplated the plastered ceiling. Why, oh, why had she allowed herself to fall for the man? A mistress. She truly was his mistress now. Why had she fallen into this trap when she knew that she wasn't the kind who wanted to share?

CHAPTER 12

Lock, Stock, and Barrel

CARRICK EYED THE DOOR THROUGH WHICH JULIET HAD VANISHED. Something clearly bothered the lass.

"Carrick?" His mother knocked louder.

He huffed an impatient breath and reached the door in three long strides, then flung it open.

His mother's lips were pressed into a thin line of disapproval. "Carrick, you must bid you guests farewell. It's the *least* you can do under the circumstances."

"Circumstances?" he repeated.

The dowager's lips parted as if to reply but then, apparently thinking better of it, she turned and swept back down the hall.

Carrick followed in a pensive mood. Juliet was downright skittish. Why? Och, the matter of the contract didn't help matters, but surely, something more bothered her.

They reached the drawing room and he began the long series of farewells, absently participating in the 'oh, let's do this again, soon' conversations to the round of 'thank you's' and a good hearty 'farewell' when he finally herded them to the door. With his thoughts revolving around Juliet, he found the torturous ritual even more tedious than usual.

Finally, the last carriage departed, and his mother headed toward her suite. Carrick turned to the stairs that led to Juliet's room.

"What happened to Juliet?" Catherine said.

He glanced over his shoulder and slowed to allow his sister to catch up with him.

"If I may say so, brother dear, your prospective brides were rather catty tonight, especially Audrey. Did you see the way she shoved Juliet into your arms? Oh, you couldn't have. You were wearing the blindfold. Well, let me assure you, Audrey was trying to be the last…"

Prospective brides. He winced. What mistress would enjoy the company of her lover's prospective brides? He'd been so eager to see her, he hadn't given her perspective thought. What a fool he'd been.

"And Mother said…" Catherine prattled in the background.

Mother. Her determination to see him wed was the root of his problem. It was time to get his mother and her interference out of his life.

An idea flashed across his mind. He reached the stairs and paused. His sister swung around the newel post at the base of the stairs. "What would you say about a trip to London and an allowance to spend?" he interrupted her stream of complaints.

From the sudden shine in her eyes, he knew her answer.

"London?" she breathed.

"And let's add a sea holiday at Brighton as well, shall we?" he suggested. That southern-most tip of England was as far away from Lennoxlove House as he could get without dropping his mother into the sea.

"Mother *loves* the sea," Catherine gasped. "Oh, it will be

wonderful, Carrick. I am so weary of the country. Mother was complaining of it herself, just yesterday."

She hurried up the stairs ahead of him, clearly headed for their mother's suite to share the news.

Carrick chuckled. Whatever money they spent would be well worth their absence. He jogged up the remaining stairs and continued up another floor to Juliet's room. Finally, they could be alone. He could hardly wait. He took the hall in long strides, his cock hardening with each step.

He reached her room and hesitated. No light shone under the door. Surely, she wasn't asleep already. He rapped softly on the door. No answer. He grasped the knob and turned. The door was unlocked. Slowly, he opened the door a crack and peeked inside.

In the dim moonlight streaming through the window, he discerned Juliet beneath the blankets on the bed. She didn't stir. Disappointment threaded through him. His cock was so hard it hurt. He stepped inside and padded to the foot of the bed, but when he caught sight of the frown etched on her face, his primal thoughts fled.

Aye, this issue of a wife had and would only worsen matters between them. He'd have to think of an arrangement that would satisfy them both. He couldn't—he *wouldn't*—lose Juliet. Not over something as trifling as a wife.

With a rueful sigh, Carrick unbuttoned his shirt. He should go to his own bed... He pushed his breeches down over his hips, then stepped out of them and slipped under the covers beside Juliet. It felt so right to have her by his side. He couldn't imagine being anywhere else.

He didn't expect to find sleep so easily, but her rhythmic breathing soothed like a lullaby, and his eyes drifted shut.

~

CARRICK AWOKE WHEN JULIET STIRRED, AND OPENED HIS EYES TO the sun cresting the tree line beyond the bedroom window. Juliet's hair fanned across the pillow and the slight frown from the night before still marred her brow. He propped onto an elbow and brushed his lips against that worry crease.

Her eyes fluttered open.

"Good morning, sweeting," he murmured.

Her face relaxed.

Carrick brushed a lock of hair from her cheek. "Shall we spend the day in bed, love?"

She laughed and the warmth in her tone made the blood surge straight to his cock. She abruptly tensed and the frown lines returned.

"There's too much sewing to be done." She sat up. The movement caused her shift to slip over her shoulder and expose her white skin.

"Forget the sewing." He settled back amongst the pillows. "Take off your shift and sit on me, lass." She glanced at the sheet, tented by his cock, and his shaft further thickened.

She sent him a sidelong glance and for a long moment he thought she meant to refuse. Then she got to her knees and ever so slowly pulled the hem of her shift up and over her shoulders.

Eyes locked with his, she tossed the garment on the floor. "I'm already late. Why not a few minutes more?"

"Minutes?" Carrick snorted, recalling her taunt that he'd last only minutes in her bed. Ah, he still had so much to teach her. He tracked his gaze over her breasts. Her nipples protruded in a way that begged to be suckled.

She shook her hair. The mass of silky strands tumbled over her shoulders as she twisted her fingers in the sheets and slowly tugged it off his body. He drew a long, ragged breath as the soft material slid over his flesh.

She didn't immediately mount him, like he wanted. Instead, she traced a finger up his thigh and chest, then back down again. Her feather-light touch along with the wait threatened to drive him mad.

"Sit on me," he demanded again.

A tiny smile played at the corner of her mouth as she swung a slim leg over his hips and straddled him. He cupped her breasts and gently squeezed. She closed her eyes and moaned. Gently, Carrick tweaked her nipples. Still, she didn't slide down onto him. Instead, she leaned into him. The curls between her legs tickled his shaft, then her mons bumped him. Pleasure streaked through him.

"I need you, lass, *please*," he begged.

She wiggled her hips. "How much?"

"Desperately." He fought the temptation to grab her hips and slam her down onto him.

"I see," she murmured, lowering her body with excruciating slowness until the tip of his shaft nudged her wet entrance. "Perhaps I should take pity on you and —"

Carrick seized her hips and shoved her down as he thrust.

She drew a sharp breath. He began to buck beneath her. He drove deeper. She braced her hands on his chest and ground down on his hard length.

Her breath quickened. Worry followed satisfaction. The way her channel closed around his cock, he wouldn't last long. He clenched his jaw and willed his desire to orgasm into submission. He slid his thumb between her wet folds and swirled it over her swollen nub. She rocked against him and he exerted herculean effort to delay his pleasure.

Her muscles abruptly went rigid and her channel tightened around him. Carrick lost control. A moan ripped from his lungs. Blinding pleasure spasmed his body and he emptied his seed deep inside her.

When the last ripple of pleasure faded, she collapsed against his chest and he cradled her close as he ran his fingers through her hair. She was so beautiful. He wanted the moment to last forever.

A sudden knock on the door caused them both to start.

"Miss Thatcher?" a maid called. "Are you awake?"

Carrick smothered a grin as Juliet slid off his body and hopped from the bed.

"Just a moment, please," she called.

He lay back on the pillows, folded his arms behind his head and watched her scramble into her shift.

Juliet hurried to the door and opened it a crack. "It's the dowager," the maid informed. "She wishes to see you in the breakfast parlor, at once."

Carrick tensed.

"She says to hurry."

Juliet promised to come immediately and closed the door. She faced Carrick, her face white. "The dowager," she whispered, and darted to the armoire to select a light green muslin day dress.

Carrick rose and scooped his breeches from the floor, then pulled them on over his hips, one eye on Juliet. She looked terrified. He scowled. Could his mother be tormenting the lass? He retrieved his shirt from the floor and tossed it on the bed before crossing to where Juliet wriggled into her gown.

"Allow me." He tied the ribbons on the back as he studied her face in the armoire's mirror. The frown lines had returned. "Don't fret so, lass. What's between us is not my mother's concern."

She lifted her eyes to his in the mirror. "I know the rules, Carrick—and I know better than to break them."

She pulled free and grabbed the brush from the vanity to give her hair a few quick strokes before turning in the mirror for a final inspection. Satisfied, she hurried back to him, rose on tiptoes, and gave him a quick peck on the check before she dashed out the door.

Carrick drew a thoughtful breath.

She knew better than to break the rules, eh?

He had to do something about that.

CHAPTER 13

Cravats and Cards

THE DOWAGER LOOKED UP FROM HER BREAKFAST OF EGGS AND toast as Juliet entered.

"Your Grace," Juliet croaked through dry lips and curtsied.

"Juliet, dear, please have a seat." The dowager nodded, indicating a chair at the table to her right. "It's time we talk."

Juliet drew a deep, shaking breath. *Time we talk*. There could be nothing good about those words. "Certainly, Your Grace," she murmured as she obediently seated herself in the indicated chair.

"You're from London, aren't you?" the dowager asked as she set her hardboiled egg in its porcelain holder and expertly cracked the shell with a spoon.

"Yes, Your Grace."

"Thatcher," the woman said thoughtfully. "The Sussex Thatchers?"

Juliet blinked. Sussex Thatchers? Puzzled, she shook her head.

"Oh? Then where does your father live?" the dowager asked.

Juliet smiled a little sadly—she'd practiced this response in the mirror a hundred times—and said, "My father...has passed away, Your Grace." It could have been the truth. Who knew?

The woman appeared surprised. "My condolences, child. And your mother?"

Juliet bit her lip, then caught the nervous action. "My mother—"

"Good morning, Mother," Carrick's deep voice interrupted.

Juliet sent him a smile of relief.

The dowager nodded at her son. "Catherine mentioned you're sending us to London." She gave her egg another whack.

"Aye. From the number of trunks I see littering the halls, you plan on taking the entire estate with you." Carrick took his seat opposite the woman.

The dowager pursed her lips, then turned to Juliet and patted her hand. "Run along, dear. We'll chat later."

Juliet blinked, surprised at the friendliness of the gesture, but she didn't have to be asked twice to leave. Studiously ignoring Carrick, she rose and hurried toward the door.

Before she reached the hallway, she caught Carrick words, "I have had enough of you interfering in my affairs," before the door closed.

Fear knotted Juliet's stomach. The dowager knew of her son's affair. She rounded a corner and ran straight into Catherine. The young girl grabbed her arms and swung her around in a dance.

"We're off tomorrow," she said, grinning from ear to ear. "Oh, please say my new gown is ready. I simply *must* wear it on holiday."

"You're leaving?" Juliet asked, surprised.

"Carrick's sending us to London," she bubbled, falling into

step as Juliet resumed her walk down the hallway. "And Brighton. Mother loves the sea. But I need my gown. Do say you can finish it before we leave tomorrow, please?"

Juliet smiled as they neared the stairs. "I'll try my best."

"Thank you, thank you a thousand times," Catherine cried. "Now, I must pack." She blew Juliet a kiss and raced up the stairs ahead of her.

Juliet watched her go with a smile and began climbing the stairs. Truth be told, she was relieved to be escaping the dowager's censorious eye—along with the promised awkward chat concerning her parents. Hopefully, the woman would be too busy readying for the trip to continue the chat. Spending the day tucked away in the sewing room hemming Catherine's gown would help ensure that happened.

The day proved busier than expected, not only with finishing Catherine's gown but with mending various day and morning dresses the dowager sent up for repair. Juliet felt sure that both the dowager and her daughter had packed every article of clothing they possessed.

Twice, Carrick dropped by. But the hustle and bustle drove him off with no more than a look—a sultry, seductive one— passing between them. Finally, the clock struck midnight, and Juliet rose stiffly from her chair. Her fingers ached, but she released a sigh of satisfaction from a job well done.

It didn't take long to tidy the room. She tossed the last spool of thread into her sewing basket and reached to shut the lid. A glimpse of silk caught her eye and she smiled as she slipped a finger over Carrick's cravat, still safely tucked away. Hopefully, he'd be waiting in her bed. As tired as she was, she would wake the moment his lips caressed her skin.

To her disappointment, she arrived to find her bed empty.

Perhaps he thought her too tired. Juliet considered seeking him in his room, but with her luck of late, she would run straight into the dowager.

With a sigh, she undressed, pulled her night rail over her shoulders and dropped into bed.

She was nearly asleep before her head touched the pillow.

～

Juliet awoke to the noon sun warming her face. She sat bolt upright, heart pounding. She'd overslept. The dowager and her daughter had left for London hours ago. She dressed in a hurry and rushed downstairs on the off chance they hadn't yet departed. The last thing she needed was for the dowager to find a reason to dislike her.

At the bottom step, she encountered one of the maids.

"The duchess? Catherine?" Juliet asked, pausing to catch her breath.

"Lordy, miss, they left at dawn," the maid replied and shuffled off.

Juliet blew out a long breath and bit her lip. Oh well. No doubt, the dowager had noticed her missing from the line of staff biding them a safe journey. She could only hope the woman would forget the matter before she saw her next.

She glanced around, noting how quiet the place seemed, then started back up the stairs. She stopped in the library, hoping to see Carrick, but the room stood empty. With a sigh, she closed the door and headed for the sewing room. The dowager and her daughter might be gone, but she still had plenty of dresses left to sew.

Juliet slowed at sight of the open sewing room door. Had she forgotten to close it last night? She entered the room and frowned. The partially sewn dresses and her sewing basket were missing. She glanced around, noting the chests of fabric missing, as well. As she slowly pivoted, her gaze snagged on her sewing basket sitting on the floor near the inner door that led to an adjoining room.

She hurried to the basket, but to her surprise, discovered it empty. Her gaze caught on a pair of scissors peeking out from the bottom of the door. As she touched the door it swung open slightly. A pincushion sat on the rug in the center of the adjoining room. Six feet farther away lay a spool of thread.

"This is exceedingly odd," she murmured and retrieved her tools, then noticed a second spool of thread near the far door.

She paused, then smiled. This was a breadcrumb trail. Carrick's doing. It had to be. With a heart growing lighter by the step, she followed the trail of pincushions, thimbles and thread spools down the servants' stairs and out a side door leading to the castle's side lawn.

The trail led across the grass. Near where the garden path vanished behind a copse of trees, a length of muslin was artfully draped over a bush. She frowned and hurried to rescue the fabric before it stained.

What was the man thinking? Still, she found herself smiling as she folded the fabric and placed it atop her sewing basket. She saw the playing cards, a line leading down the center of the path and disappearing behind the trees.

She'd missed him the night before. Her smile widened as she followed the trail, collecting the cards along the way until the path gave way to a private garden. A gazebo nestled under an ancient oak, and Carrick practiced archery nearby, wearing only a white shirt and a pair of form-fitting, dark gray breeches.

She paused to admire his muscular buttocks and powerful thighs. Her fingers itched to slide over those firm, warm muscles. She'd never thought of a man's buttocks and thighs as particularly fascinating before.

He bent to remove an arrow from a quiver lying on a table and she watched the shift and flex of his thigh muscle before wrenching her eyes away. A throb pulsed between her thighs.

He lowered his bow and she lifted her gaze to his face. His

eyebrow raised in amusement. Heavens, she could only be glad he wasn't privy to her thoughts. He'd be prancing around the estate in smug satisfaction for a week—maybe longer.

A mischievous grin crossed his face as he crooked a finger and motioned for her to join him. When she arrived, he took the sewing basket and set it on the ground as she eyed the target, taking note of the half-dozen arrows clustered around the bullseye.

"You have astonishing marksmanship," she said.

A humorous glint entered his eye. "Aye, my shaft is hard and its aim true."

She jerked her eyes back to his, forcing herself not to look at his crotch. The man was shameless. She couldn't prevent a smile. then recalled that she'd overslept. "I fear I failed in bidding the duchess and Catherine farewell," she confessed.

He chuckled. "Mother insisted you catch up on your rest. She wasn't offended, if that's what concerns you."

That was difficult to believe, but she smiled anyway. "Well, I'm well rested now."

His eyebrow lifted as he reached past her to prop his bow against the gazebo's nearest wall. He murmured, "For now, aye?"

She lowered her lashes.

"I found a most curious item in your sewing basket." He bent and retrieved something from his quiver.

His cravat. She took the fabric, suddenly tongue-tied.

"You kept it," he said.

She lifted her eyes to his. Slowly, he lowered his lips to hers. He smelled of fresh air and the sandalwood spice of his cravat. She closed her eyes and melted into his embrace, a thrilling kiss soft, tender, and sweet.

A kiss that ended far too soon.

He pulled away and she opened her mouth to object, but he surprised her by swinging her up into his arms.

"I'm of a mind to taste your charms, lass." He peered down at her through hooded eyes. "Here. Now."

She shivered. "Here?"

He carried her into the gazebo and lay her on a plaid spread across the weathered wooden floor.

"Carrick," she said with mock sternness.

He shrugged and dropped down by her side. Objections died on her lips as he covered her lips and sucked her tongue into his mouth. A sizzle of heat shot through her inner core and clenched her sex.

He loosened her chignon and threaded his fingers through her curls as he kissed a path from her lips to her neck before pausing to suck the tender flesh beneath her ear. She slid her hands over his arms. Muscle shifted beneath her fingers as his palm skimmed her waist. He covered a breast and kneaded the soft flesh. Heat pooled in her belly. She arched her hips.

"You're more than ready, aren't you?" He chuckled.

"Take me," she whispered.

He rose to his knees, rucked up her dress, then slipped her under drawers down and off.

"Open your legs for me, lass," he murmured as he leaned over and kissed her eyes closed.

She obliged, enjoying the heightened sensations of his lips as he planted another line of kisses along her jawline and down her throat.

She tensed in anticipation of him levering himself over her. A warm hand clasped her thigh. A quiver radiated through her stomach. He clasped her other thigh and Juliet shivered. The man was a magician. She discerned the shift of his weight on her legs, then gasped when warm lips closed over her sex.

Juliet shoved upright, then froze at sight of Carrick's head between her legs. While she'd heard plenty of Aphrodite's ladies speak of taking a man's member into their mouths, she'd never heard of a man doing the same to a woman. His tongue flicked her engorged nub. Pleasure rocketed through her.

"Carrick," she breathed.

He shifted so that he could look at her, but his mouth continued its wicked work. She squirmed when he sucked her. He laughed against her flesh. The sound tickled heightened senses.

"Lay back and close your eyes, lass. Let me please you."

Please her? Close her eyes? He suckled harder. She didn't think she could tear her gaze from his dark head buried between her thighs even if she wanted to. He drew his tongue from the base of her channel, up through her wet folds and circled her sex.

A wordless whimper escaped her lips. Pleasure mounted. He wrapped his arms around her thighs and pulled her tighter against his mouth. Palms flat on the floorboard, she closed her eyes, braced herself and pulsed against him.

Her orgasm exploded through her, stealing her breath as her body spasmed, the force of her pleasure ripping a cry from her. "Carrick. Oh, God, Carrick."

Juliet collapsed back against the wood. He stroked her until the last shudder subsided, leaving her weak-kneed. "I couldn't last long," she whispered, feeling uncharacteristically shy.

He chuckled and straightened. "Your passion is what I love most about you, Juliet."

Love. The word slipped from his tongue so naturally, yet hung in the air between them like lead.

He unbuttoned his breeches. His engorged member sprang free. Her heart pounded. He settled between her legs and buried himself inside her to the hilt. Juliet wrapped her arms around his neck as he thrust with increasing urgency. His breath bathed her flesh where neck met shoulder. Shivers raced across her flesh. His breath hitched. Pleasure rippled through her. He thrust harder and groaned as her channel flooded with his seed.

Her heart thundered. She would never get enough of this man. He stroked slower and a strange sense of need rippled through her. The unexpected need to cry surfaced. Juliet buried her face in his shoulder until, at last, he relaxed. He breathed deep, his chest expanding against hers. Juliet tightened her hold around his neck in the moment before he rose onto his elbows. He caught her chin with his hand and kissed her slow and tender. Finally, he broke the kiss and rolled off her, then propped himself up on an elbow.

Gently, he ran his fingers through her hair before he tucked a curl behind her ear. "Now that we have Lennoxlove House to ourselves, I'll be making love to you in every room and against every tree."

She lifted her eyebrows and laughed. "We're surrounded by a forest, Carrick."

His grin softened into a warm smile. "Then we'll be busy, won't we?"

CHAPTER 14

A Decision

Love. CARRICK HAD NEVER UTTERED THAT WORD IN A WOMAN'S presence before. In fact, he'd taken great care to avoid it. With Juliet, the word flowed effortlessly from his lips. At first, he'd thought his mother had planted the fool notion in his head. She'd surprised him that day in the breakfast parlor. He'd opened his mouth to inform her he would no longer entertain her matchmaking attempts, but she'd announced she no longer felt her services were needed on that particular subject now that he'd found love.

Love. He'd thought his mother quite mad, but now, he was no longer so certain.

The more he thought about Juliet, the more he found the word suited her.

"You're not paying attention," Juliet's scold shattered his thoughts.

Carrick lifted an eyebrow. They lay in her bed with the

early afternoon sun slanting through her bedroom window. Of late, they'd taken to playing cards and wagering articles of clothing, but he'd yet to win. Today would certainly be no different. He had only his shirt left while Juliet had only lost her under drawers.

He grinned. On the angle in which he lay, he had a fine view of her white thighs.

"Focus, Carrick." Juliet laughed, even as she opened her legs to provide him an even more distracting view.

Indeed, how could he focus on the cards? She had his full attention.

"It's time to show your hand," she said.

He lay his cards face up on the bed. Three jacks and a deuce.

Juliet snorted and tilted the cards in her slim fingers. Queens. Four of them. It was the third time he'd seen them that round.

"You're cheating," he said.

"Am I?"

She said the words with such confidence that he momentarily wondered if he'd erred. "Well, aren't you?"

"You're asking? Then you can't prove a thing." She giggled.

He rolled his eyes. How could a man concentrate on anything save her luscious body? He should have known never to second guess himself.

She dropped the cards on the bed and nodded at his shirt. "Take it off."

Och. As usual, he was the first one naked...but not for long.

As he unfastened his buttons, she rose from the bed and lifted the lid of her sewing basket, which rested on the bedside table. She pulled his cravat from the basket, turned back to him and ordered, "Lay back and close your eyes."

He lifted a brow but obeyed, his cock hardening even more. "As you wish, my love."

There it was again. Love.

Juliet didn't seem to notice. She laughed and hurried around to his side of the bed, then leaned over and tied the cravat like a blindfold.

Her breasts brushed his shoulder. He reached for the soft mounds, but she evaded his grasp. "Now, now, don't move, Carrick. Not yet."

The perfume of her hair floated around him. She smelled like roses. The soft rustle of cloth told him she undressed. The thought only heightened his need.

A delicate finger touched his shoulder then trailed down the center line of his chest and circled the base of his cock before she wrapped her small hands about his cock. He shuddered in anticipation, but then a thought crossed his mind.

"Tell me, lass, did you have this in mind when you claimed my cravat at the Midnight Ball?"

She gave a quiet laugh, then murmured in a low, sultry tone, "No. I intended to win the wager and be rid of you."

Her soft, wet lips closed over the tip of his cock as she drew several inches of his length into her mouth and began to suck.

He groaned. "What a luscious mouth," he gasped.

Slowly, she licked the length of him, before once again arriving at the tip. He drew a sharp breath and fought for control, but to no avail. He pumped faster. Pleasure—need—rushed to the surface. He *needed* her. His breath hitched as his orgasm started to crest. God help him, she was merciless. Carrick yanked his member from her mouth and ripped the blindfold from his face.

She knelt on the bed, naked. With a growl, he flipped her onto the mattress and mounted her. She arched into him and, to his surprise, within half a dozen strokes, she whimpered with pleasure. In seconds, his orgasm shuddered through him.

Carrick threw back his head and filled her to the brim. As the last ripples of pleasure subsided, he slid aside and held her close. They lay, drowsy and sated.

Never in his wildest dreams had he thought to find a woman who could match his passion stride for stride. Just as tantalizing, her mind was sharp.

He had to do something about that damn contract, and soon. A year was not long enough.

He needed Juliet to be his mistress—for a lifetime.

Realization struck with an intensity that took his breath, then settled over him as natural as breathing. There was only one solution: he had to marry her.

That presented a challenge. Not due to her lack of noble birth, but from her madam of a mother. Surely, he could find a way past that world-wise warden.

Sleep blurred the edges of his consciousness. If anyone could help him dance through this mire of the heart, it would be Sir Stirling James.

∼

Two weeks later, Stirling entered Carrick's library. "My dear fellow," he boomed in a laughing voice as he strode through the door. "I have come to collect my prized stallion."

Carrick closed the book he'd been reading and rose from his desk. "I should have known you would come yourself. You've an uncanny talent for matchmaking. I should never have doubted you."

Both men laughed and clapped each other on the back.

A maid entered carrying a silver tray with a decanter and two full glasses of claret. They settled comfortably in high-backed mahogany wing chairs near the window and the maid set the tray on the small rosewood table between them.

Carrick took a glass and raised it in salute. "Something special I just received from France," he said.

Stirling picked up the remaining glass. He leaned forward and rested his elbows on his knees. "I've found a solution for your problem, Carrick. Well, several solutions, as you have more than one problem."

His friend drained his claret and returned the empty glass to the tray. "France," he said in a tone of finality. "It just so happens that Victor de Balzac, playwright extraordinaire, has had difficulties finding a passionate enough woman to, shall we say, satisfy his needs. I have discovered that Madam Aphrodite has always dreamt of living there as a woman of means..." He let his voice trail off.

Carrick snorted. If Juliet's mother was a tenth as passionate as her daughter, then Victor de Balzac would live the remainder of his life a very happy man. "What does Madam Aphrodite have to say about this?" he queried.

"The deed is already done," Stirling assured with a laugh. "They became besotted the moment they met. One of the best matches I've ever made. She's off to France, though you have agreed to see her girls settled."

"How many dowries am I financing?" he asked dryly.

"A small fortune." Stirling offered a droll smile. "Count yourself lucky there is nothing your money will not buy."

Carrick shrugged. To secure Juliet's hand in marriage, he would sign over his estate. The thought of spending nights carousing and gambling at card tables had lost all appeal.

"When will you ask her?" Stirling asked.

"Soon," Carrick murmured.

A smile played over his lips. The time had come to play another round of cards.

CHAPTER 15

Queen of Hearts

JULIET SMILED AT CATHERINE AS THE GIRL SPUN BEFORE THE mirror.

"You have such talent, Juliet," Catherine cried, obviously thrilled to have returned from London to find yet another creation waiting in the sewing room, this one a blue-sprigged muslin day dress with green satin trim. "It's beautiful. I'm not taking it off. I'm wearing it now. It's beautiful."

Juliet smiled as she removed the pins from her mouth and jammed them one-by-one into the pincushion resting beside her on the carpet.

"I quite agree," Carrick's deep baritone approved from the doorway. "Join us for dinner, my dear."

Juliet glanced over her shoulder. He stood in the doorway, looking as handsome as ever in dark gray breeches.

"Please, do come," Catherine chimed in before skipping to

her brother. She placed a kiss on his cheek, then hurried past him and disappeared down the hall.

Carrick crossed to Juliet and extended a hand. She placed her fingers in his and he pulled her to her feet—then yanked her into his arms. "I agree with Catherine," he said, holding her tightly. "Join us."

She suppressed a sigh. Now that the dowager and Catherine had returned, the parade of wife candidates would resume. The thought rankled more than ever.

"I can't, not when I have so much hemming to do." She pulled his head down to hers and gave him a sound kiss, then twisted out of his arms.

Carrick lunged for her, then straightened when his mother's voice sounded in the hall. "Carrick? Carrick, my dear, the guests have arrived."

"Dinner. Please," he whispered, catching her hand and planting a kiss on her fingertips.

She shook her head.

"Join me with the gentlemen at cards after dinner tonight in the study." He pulled her into his arms again. "Afterwards, we shall enjoy more of this. Hmmm? I would see you wearing your mask and nothing else."

"Or your cravat?" She smiled up and fluttered her dark lashes. They had discovered many delightful uses for his cravats.

"Yes."

"Carrick?" The dowager's voice sounded much closer.

"Damn." He released her and hurried from the room.

The day flew. Juliet finished a riding jacket for Catherine, stopping only to enjoy a quick snack of toast slathered with fresh butter and topped with marmalade.

At last, the sun set, and she returned to her room to ready herself for an evening of cards. She often played cards with Carrick in bed, although they rarely finished a game, and while she'd discovered him to be a card cheat in his own right, she still held the edge.

She picked up her white Venetian mask and turned it over in her hands before tying it to the bedpost, imagining the enjoyment it would provide later. Juliet perused the selection of gowns in the armoire, skipping over those with the provocative bodices that Carrick preferred, and selected a peach taffeta with white satin rosettes adorning the scooped neckline. Finally, she paused before the mirror, gave her ringlets one last pat, then headed for the door.

By the time she reached the study, a group of gentlemen lounged about the card table. The gentlemen rose immediately and Carrick invited her to join them.

"Gentlemen, may I introduce Juliet Thatcher," Carrick said, then turning to the two silver-haired gentlemen, continued, "Lord Haynes and Mr. Lamont." Lastly, he nodded at the portly young man who was clearly awestruck by her breasts. "And Mr. Thaddeus Turnby."

Juliet dipped a polite curtsey and took her seat. The men followed suit.

"I shall deal," Carrick announced.

While the gentlemen murmured agreement, she smiled and prepared for an enjoyable evening. As they played, she watched her opponents, observing and cataloging their expressions and ticks as the rounds played out.

By the third game, she'd determined that only the elderly Mr. Lamont possessed any sort of skill. She eyed Carrick as he dealt another hand, puzzled as to why he'd asked her to join their card game.

As they picked up their cards, Juliet glanced down at hers. Queens. All four. She blinked in surprise and glanced up into Carrick's amused face. Clearly, he'd dealt her a winning hand. She frowned, wondering why, as the men looked at their cards and placed their chips.

As Mr. Lamont raised a hand to knock on the table, Carrick lifted a finger.

"Wait," he said. "I'd like to add this."

They watched as he drew a parchment torn in half from his breast pocket and laid it down over the bets.

"I say, what's this?" the portly Lord Haynes asked.

"Wait." Carrick locked gazes with Juliet, then withdrew something from his front pocket and dropped it on top of the paper.

Juliet froze.

The hereditary Hamilton engagement ring glinted in the chandelier light. Her eyes snagged on the heading of the paper and she recognized her contract...torn in half. Her heart pounded. Surely, he wasn't foolish enough to propose to her? This was no ordinary card game. Her throat tightened.

She looked up at him.

He leaned back and rested an elbow on one of the armrests, then lifted a brow as if daring her to decline the offer.

"What have we here?" The old gentleman raised his hand to give the table a rap.

Juliet shoved to her feet. "I withdraw from the round."

Carrick slowly arose.

"By Jove, lass," Mr. Lamont chuckled. "That's not how commerce is played."

"Then his grace is fortunate," she said.

"Hardly," Carrick murmured.

Juliet whirled and raced from the room.

"Wait!" he called.

She ran. He caught up with her at the stairs, reaching for her, but she evaded his grasp and ran up them as fast she could.

"Juliet, why? You owe me an answer," he shouted.

He was right. Juliet stopped on the landing and backed toward the wall. He stopped two stairs beneath her and stared straight into her eyes.

"You know quite well I can never accept that ring," she said in a shaky voice.

"Why not?" he demanded.

"Don't be absurd," she snapped. "I'm no lady. I possess no title or money. How can I marry you? The difference in our social standing is far too great." She clenched her hands and fought tears. "I am your mistress, Carrick. A gentleman does not marry his mistress."

He started to reply.

Juliet shook her head. "Please, no more."

She gathered her skirts and fled to her room. After locking the door, she threw herself headlong onto her bed and wailed.

He knocked on her door. Several times. She begged him to leave. He left with the promise that they would speak in the morning.

An hour later, Juliet took a deep breath and sat up, looking down at the cards crumpled in her hand. She knew now what she had to do, before the situation grew worse for the both of them. What made her think she could succeed as a mistress?

She penned a letter, begging him to forget her. Of course, society would never let her marry him, regardless of how he might feel. But now, she knew she couldn't survive him marrying someone else. The thought of him making love to another woman would break her heart. She held nothing back, ending with a last line that conveyed the truth she'd been hiding all along: *I can never share you with another woman, and thus, I can no longer be your mistress.*

With that, she packed a canvas bag with her belongings, including the crumpled cards from the game. After the castle occupants retired, she slipped into the dark hall. She'd purchase fare at the village coaching inn and be gone before anyone thought to look for her.

∾

SEVEN DAYS LATER, JULIET EXITED THE MAIL COACH AND trudged up the cobblestone street toward Lady Aphrodite's House of Pleasure. She'd taken the fastest coach to London she could find, but they'd met with more than one setback along the way, which delayed the coach's arrival until after dark on the seventh day. It didn't matter. Her mother didn't expect her. There had been no point in writing a letter that would have arrived at the same day and time she did.

She'd thought of Carrick the entire journey. Her heart twisted, knowing he could never truly be hers. Finally, she turned at the wrought iron fence. Lady Aphrodite's house stood before her, but instead of lights twinkling cheerfully in the windows, all but one stood dark. Where strains of music had floated through the front rooms, silence reigned.

Juliet ran to the door and twisted the brass knob. "Ma? Ma?" She darted inside.

A single taper in a pewter holder rested on the floor, illuminating an empty room—save a single chair upon which her mother sat, chin on her chest.

Her mother jerked awake and jumped to her feet. "There you are, at last, child." She smiled widely and held out her arms.

Juliet frowned. "What happened?" She glanced around the empty room. "Where are the girls? The furnishings? Is there trouble with the law?"

Her mother enveloped her in a hug and chuckled. "The girls have gone and married, and the same for me, as well, love. The duke and I thought it wiser if I left without a fuss." She pinched Juliet's cheeks. "You shouldn't be here. Not after how hard we've worked to whitewash your past. Why, I only came back here tonight because he fetched me. He's distraught, the poor boy. You're lucky you came when you did. Come morning, and I would've sailed with the tide to France."

"France?" Juliet repeated in utter disbelief. "Whatever are you speaking of?"

"Lawks, child, I'm a proper wife now, wed in a church. Sir Stirling and your duke found me a husband. We thought I should stay there for a week. You know, until things are settled and everyone thinks I've always lived in France." She winked.

Juliet frowned, more confused than ever.

"And not only me, the girls as well, every one of them wed with a proper dowry." Her mother waved her hands to indicate the empty room. "All for you, Juliet. When I return from France, no one will think to connect me with this place. They've made us respectable. There's naught to fear." She pulled a folded paper from her bodice and rolled her eyes. "Have I taught you nothing, girl? Gone and torn your contract? Really, now, though it's hard to be angry with you." She clucked her tongue.

Juliet stumbled to the chair and sat down, her mother's words starting to sink in. Whitewash her past? Thousands of pounds in dowries? Her gaze fell on the torn contract in her mother's hands.

"Where did you get that?" The last time she'd seen it, it lay atop a mound of chips on a card table.

"Where else?" Her mother snorted.

"Carrick?" Juliet swallowed. "Here?" Of course, her mother had said that, hadn't she?

"Rode his horse straight here after fetching me to help find you," her mother said. "The boy hasn't slept in days. I put him up in the Swan Room. It's the only one left with a bed—"

Juliet stopped listening.

She raced up the stairs and down the hall to the third door on the right. The door stood open enough to reveal a guttering candle and the shape of a man lying on his back with his arm flung over his face, a booted foot hanging off the bed.

Carrick.

She halted in the doorway and stared at him for a long

moment, then turned on her heel and fled back down the stairs to where she'd dropped her canvas bag on the floor.

"Juliet, wait." Her mother grabbed her hand and tilted her face up to meet her eyes. "The man loves you, child. Don't be a fool and throw it away. He's fixed it all so you can marry him. Put good hard coin where his mouth is."

It was the highest compliment her mother could pay.

Juliet took a deep breath, her heart growing lighter by the moment. "I know, Ma." She rummaged through her bag until she finally found what she sought.

"Then you'll marry him?" her mother demanded. "My daughter…a lady—a duchess?"

The pride in her mother's voice was hard to miss. "Not because he's a duke, Ma." No. It had nothing to do with a title. It never had. She couldn't live without him, just as he obviously couldn't live without her. She'd be a fool to throw it away— especially when she felt the same.

"Well, you can love him if you want," her mother called as she ran back up the stairs. "As long as the outcome is the same."

Juliet hurried back up the stairs and down the hallway. She slipped back into the bedroom, softly closing the door behind her.

He still lay asleep on the bed.

Slowly, she unbuttoned his shirt and breeches, keeping an eye on his slow, steady breathing. In the dim light, she could see exhaustion on his face. He'd clearly ridden hard, but then, perhaps the exhaustion on his face had more to do with dealing with her mother. She quickly unpinned her hair, shook it over her shoulders, and then pushed her gown from her shoulders. The fabric pooled to the floor. Slowly, she climbed onto the bed and straddled him.

He awoke with a start and started to straighten, but Juliet pushed him back down.

"Juliet." His gaze dropped to her breasts, the apex at her legs, then lifted back to her face. "Marry me, lass. I beg you."

His manhood stirred and began to harden beneath her sex. With a smile, she guided his shaft into her wet entrance, sinking down on him fully as she revealed the crumpled cards that she'd retrieved from her canvas bag. Queen by queen, she dropped them onto his chest, ending last with the queen of hearts.

"My beautiful duchess." He gave her a tender smile—then flipped her onto her back. She squeaked, then gasped when he drove into her.

She wrapped her legs around his hips and clung to him with all her might.

"You are mine," he growled, and thrust deep.

Yes. She was his.

SNEAK PEEK AT REDEMPTION OF A MARQUESS

Redemption of a Marquess
The Marriage Maker
Book Seven
Rules of Refinement

Tarah Scott
Erin Rye

She insisted on saving him... He let her.

Valan Grey, the 6th Earl of Edmonds, the Marquess of Northington, has no wish to sire an heir. His three-year-old nephew will carry on the title. His fertile sister has already borne her husband another son and a daughter for good luck. The title is safe. So why marry?

Miss Jeanine Matheson has graduated from Lady Peddington's School for Young Ladies. Only, Jeanine isn't interested in finding a husband—at least, not a young healthy husband. She aspires to become a businesswoman like Lady Peddington. All she needs is a very rich, very elderly gentleman to marry her and then, well…pass on to his reward.

CHAPTER 1

VALAN GREY, THE 6ᵀᴴ EARL OF EDMONDS, THE MARQUESS OF Northington, sipped wine and watched the brown-haired beauty waltz with Mr. Evans, a peacock amid a glittering barnyard of hens. Evans had twice stepped on her toes, yet her smile hadn't faltered. Valan slowed his stroll and spared a glance for the other wolf, almost a pup, that prowled near the open balcony doors. A breeze ruffled the young man's styled blond locks. The youth of today relied far too much on well-made coats and coiffured hair in an effort to catch a lady's attention. Any man of worth understood that what lay beneath the coat mattered far more to a lady of taste. He returned his attention to the beauty. Her partner turned to the music. Valan winced. Evans' step was off by half a beat.

Between pale satin dresses, the swirl of the beauty's emerald velvet skirt molded around her firm buttocks before she was lost from view in the sea of dancers. Had Lady Peddington suggested the dress? The beauty certainly stood out amongst the demure pastels that flared on the dance floor. She was older than the others who attended the Midnight Ball. *Perfect.* Tomorrow, he would send a letter of thanks to Honoria for her invitation to the soiree. She had a knack for knowing just the right lady for a gentleman.

Above the music and murmur of guests, a female gasp was followed by a man's curse. Valan glanced left, toward the small commotion, but a half-closed curtain hid the man and woman in the alcove. He shifted his gaze back to the dance floor. A blur in the corner of his eye registered an instant too late, and a woman collided with him. Wine sloshed over the rim of his glass and onto his crisply pressed, ivory silk waistcoat. He seized the lady's wrist to stop her fall.

Valan glanced down at the now ruined waistcoat, then met the young woman's wide-eyed gaze. "I assume you learned enough etiquette at Lady Peddington's to know that it's bad manners to collide with guests. Or is this your way of gaining an introduction?"

Her brown eyes flicked to the wine-stained waistcoat then back to his face. The fear in her gaze flashed into annoyance. "I do not want an introduction."

"Where is that bitch?" A large man lunged past the alcove curtain, half limping.

Valan deftly sidestepped him, pulling the young woman with him. Viscount Hesston stumbled two paces, narrowly missing two ladies. They cast him frowns and hurried past as he whirled.

He came up short when his gaze met Valan's. "What the devil are you doing here, Northington? Didn't think this sort of place was one of your usual haunts." The music ended and the last words were overloud in the absence of the orchestra. The viscount's eyes narrowed on the young woman. "Looking for another victim, little pigeon?" He grabbed for her.

Valan tugged her out of her assailant's reach. "This 'little pigeon' is otherwise engaged."

The man's face contorted in rage. "She is mine. I've spent the evening with her. She *owes* me."

Valan glanced where he'd last seen the beauty on the dance floor. Gone. No doubt, claimed by the young wolf. With a sigh, he returned his attention to Hesston. "Ownership is a matter of perspective. As she has ruined a very expensive waistcoat, I believe she *owes* me."

She tugged in an effort to break free. Valan held tight and nodded at a passing waiter.

"My claim supersedes yours," Hesston said as the waiter stopped beside them.

Valan set his wine glass on the waiter's tray.

"I d-do no' belong to either of y-you," the girl said.

The waiter frowned. Valan ignored him and turned curious eyes on her. "Where are you from, child?"

"That is none of your c-concern," she said.

"Perhaps not," he replied, "but indulge me."

She shook her head.

"Would you rather go with this man?" He nodded at Hesston, whose face reddened.

"She is mine," the viscount growled.

"Patience," Valan said. "She may choose to go with you, in which case I will not interfere."

"You have no right to interfere, at all," Hesston snapped.

Valan turned cold eyes on him. "Even you can wait sixty seconds." He looked at the girl and lifted a brow in question.

She glanced at Hesston, then looked back at him and shook her head. "N-nae."

"There you have it," he said. "Even at Lady Peddington's Midnight Ball, a lady is free to choose her companions."

Hesston cast a disgruntled look at her. "Dumb bitch," he muttered.

She lifted her chin. "I would rather be dumb than cruel."

The remark earned her a disdainful look from a woman strolling by on the arm of a man.

Hesston again lunged for her. Valan stepped between them.

"You're drunk, Hesston. Go home before you irritate the wrong person."

"Like you?" he sneered.

Valan shrugged. "I am not the best shot in Edinburgh."

"Damn right, you're not," he growled.

"I am more likely to set a runner on you," he said.

Hesston's eyes widened. "They hunt criminals. I have never committed a crime in my life."

"That is a matter of perspective."

A vicious glint lit Hesston's eyes. "If that is so, then one might contend that you stepped outside the law on at least *one* occasion. Last I heard, marriage to an underage woman is against the law," Hesston said.

Ah, the viscount had heard that Valan's old nemesis had returned to Edinburgh just today. Gossip traveled fast when *Society* smelled blood.

Valan gave a bland smile. "Then I am fortunate not to have committed that crime."

"You tried hard enough," Hesston declared.

"Even I do not always succeed," Valan remarked.

"You succeeded at winning your fortune in a card game," he snarled. "That is highly illegal."

"A friendly game of cards is never illegal," Valan said, then added before he could reply, "The important point to remember, my dear viscount, is that runners give an ear to high-ranking peers."

The man's face twisted into a scowl. "You think well of yourself."

Valan angled his head." I am on excellent terms with Bow Street."

Hesston took a step back. "You pay them well, is what you mean." He sneered at the girl. "A bit of muslin isn't worth this much trouble."

"I am no bit of muslin," the girl retorted.

Hesston turned, stumbled past a group of men, then hurried away.

Valan looked down at the young lady. "You cost me a great deal tonight."

Her brow furrowed. "The cost of that waistcoat is a pittance for a man like you."

He thought of the brown-haired beauty. "Money is not the only thing of worth in this world, child."

"I am no' a child."

He arched a brow. "Pray tell, how old are you?"

"Nineteen."

"A nineteen-year-old girl who nearly got herself accosted by a rather nasty viscount."

"Release me." She yanked the wrist he still gripped.

He started when something pricked his wrist. Valan drew her hand upward. She yanked harder and nearby guests glanced their way. Valan offered them a chilly smile, then urged the girl back three paces nearer the alcove.

"I beg your pardon," she began, then broke off when he tightened his grip.

He turned her hand over and forced her fingers apart. A modest diamond stick pin balanced halfway across her palm.

Valan looked at her and raised a questioning brow. "That is a gentleman's pin, if I am not mistaken."

Her mouth thinned in a mutinous line.

"Shall I call Viscount Hesston back and ask if he has lost a diamond pin?" he asked.

Her mouth parted in a small gasp. "Nae. D-do not do that. Please."

Valan released her. "I assume, then, the good viscount did not give this to you as a token of his, er, undying love?"

"Undying love?" she scoffed. "That man loves only himself."

He repressed a smile. "Forgive me, but I am curious as to how you came to be in possession of his pin. It's unlikely he removed it in order to disrobe. Removal of his cravat would not be necessary to—"

"He did not give it to me," she cut in.

"Then you slipped it from his cravat when he kissed you?"

She lifted her chin. "Ladies do not allow strange men to kiss them."

"How wonderful to know you recognize some conduct befitting a lady. I suggest you remember that when next a man asks you to accompany him to an alcove."

She dropped her gaze. Ah, he had her. She slanted a look up at him through her lashes and it was easy to see why she had captured Hesston's attention. Her innocence was a lure few men could resist. She extended a hand toward him and stepped forward. Then tripped. She cried out and collided with him. His lapel tugged downward when she grabbed him and Valan caught her.

He set her at arm's length. "That is the second time this evening you have landed in my arms." He tugged his cravat back into place, then felt the knot in an effort to assess the damage. "Perhaps we should be formally introduced before a third *encounter*?" Valan paused, then felt along the length of the cravat. His pin— He lowered his hands to his sides and leveled an assessing gaze on her. "My pin, please."

Her eyes sparkled as she opened her left hand. His ruby pin lay on her palm.

Valan took the pin. "It is not often I am shocked, but you have managed to shock me."

The laughter in her eyes vanished and her back went ramrod straight. "A gentleman would give me a head start."

He paused while slipping both pins into the front pocket of his coat. "A head start?"

"Before you call Bow Street."

A corner of his mouth twitched again, harder. He removed

his hand from his pocket. "You are safe, my child. I do not put Bow Street on the scent of young ladies."

She studied him as if uncertain, then her expression cleared and she flashed a brilliant smile. "You are kind—despite the austere face." Before he could reply, she added, "Admit it, once you discovered the pin missing, you would have assumed you lost it by accident and would no' have suspected me—just as that evil viscount will not."

"Fortune favors you on that score," Valan said. "Hesston would not hesitate to have you arrested—if, that is, you failed to comply with his demands."

She frowned. "Demands? Oh, you mean, he would make me his mistress."

"Nothing so elevated as that, but never mind. Dare I ask how you came to have this, er, talent?"

She shrugged, but a steel determination underlay the nonchalance. "A woman develops skills necessary to survive."

"Aye," he agreed. "Women are very adept at surviving. I take it, then, you need the money."

She frowned. "I do not steal for money. Well, not for myself. By-the-by, please return my pin."

He lifted a brow. "*Your* pin?"

"It certainly isn't yours," she said.

"Neither is it yours," he said.

"Finders keepers."

"Is that what you call your talent, 'finding'?"

She scowled. "You do not need it."

"My dear, if you pawn this pin, you will surely find yourself hunted by Bow Street. Unless—tell me, have you already a relationship with a pawn broker?"

She gave him a haughty stare. "I do not."

"Then we shall not begin now."

She shook her head. "Everyone thinks they know what is best for me. I don't not want—"

Valan grimaced. "Pray, say no more. Surely, Miss Peddington taught you not to use double negatives in a sentence."

She dropped her gaze. "Aye, she did."

"Will you throw away every penny your father spent to send you here by speaking like a common fishwife?"

"M-my mother sent me here."

Valan regarded her. "Do you only stutter when you're afraid?"

Her cheeks reddened even as her chin lifted. "I cannot help it. If you don't like it—" her cheeks pinked more "—then you are no gentleman."

"Your judgment of what constitutes a gentleman is sorely misguided." She opened her mouth to reply, but he lifted a hand, palm out. "Please, we will save that discussion for another time. I happen to agree. You cannot help the stutter. You can, however, choose the words you speak. I suggest you make a habit of choosing them more carefully."

Valan recognized the tall man who approached. "Wedded bliss losing its luster so soon?" Valan asked when Sir Stirling James reached them.

Stirling grinned. "Not at all." He looked pointedly at the young lady.

"I cannot make introductions," Valan said. "I don't know the young lady's name."

"Then allow me." Stirling bowed. "Miss Jeanine Matheson, I am Sir Stirling James, and this is his Lordship, the Marquess of Northington."

She extended her hand and Valan bowed over it. "A marquess?" she said. "You did not tell me you were a peer."

"You did not ask," he said, then looked at Stirling. "Do you know all the young ladies? Never say you come here often."

Stirling shook his head. "I saw ye two together. Lady Peddington told me who she was."

"Ah," Valan intoned. "It is Lady Peddington you came to visit."

"Honoria and I are old friends," Stirling said. "Not *that* kind of old friends," he added when Valan started to reply. "But if we were, the past is the past."

Valan angled his head. "As you say."

"You knew Lady Peddington before she started the school?" Miss Matheson asked.

Stirling smiled. "Indeed, I did."

"I want to have a school like this someday," she said.

"Good God, why?" Valan asked.

"To be an independent woman. Lady Peddington says a lady will do best if she finds a nice gentleman to care for her. But that is not what she did. She started the school. She makes her own money and spends it any way she pleases."

"Much responsibility comes with running a business," Valan said.

She waved her hand dismissively. "Running a gentleman's household is just as big a responsibility."

"When a lady has a gentleman to look after her, she has someone to care for her should something go wrong," he said.

She frowned. "I have known too many ladies whose husbands do not take care of them."

"She has you there, Northington," Stirling said.

"That she does," Valan said. "On that note, I shall say goodnight."

"Leaving so early?" Stirling asked.

"Aye. The hunt is finished for tonight." He looked at the young lady. "Good evening, Miss Matheson."

She took a step toward him. "Must you go?"

He flashed a bland smile. "Old gentlemen need their rest."

She grimaced. "You are not old."

"Old enough."

"The choice of gentlemen to dance with has dwindled," she said. "I thought perhaps…"

"Perhaps his lordship will dance with you." He nodded at Stirling.

She frowned at Stirling. "Lordship? You introduced yourself as Sir Stirling James."

"He is both," Valan said. "The marquess suffers an unnatural modesty. He seldom admits his title."

"The title is a courtesy, and hardly signifies," Stirling said.

Valan glimpsed Hesston talking with Lady Peddington near the far right wall, not far from a cluster of ladies. Valan returned his attention to Miss Matheson. "The marquess is probably the only gentleman present. If, that is, he's still a gentleman."

Stirling chuckled. "You would have to ask Chastity."

"Chastity?" she asked.

"His wife," Valan said.

"You're married?" The young lady wrinkled her nose. "Then it will not do for me to dance with you."

"You are refreshingly forthright," Stirling said.

"She is naïve," Valan said. "A married man has his uses."

She narrowed her eyes. "Are you married?"

"Nae, and I have no wish to be. Goodnight, Miss Matheson. Sir Stirling." He bowed and left.

www.scarsdalepublishing.com